THE
DOOR
IN THE
GARDEN
WALL

THE
DOOR
IN THE
GARDEN
WALL

SHARON J. SEIDER

XULON PRESS ELITE

Xulon Press Elite
2301 Lucien Way #415
Maitland, FL 32751
407.339.4217
www.xulonpress.com

EXULON ELITE

Paperback ISBN-13: 978-1-6628-4349-5
Ebook ISBN-13: 978-1-6628-4350-1

Dedication

*T*his story is written for our grandchildren and all children growing up in the New Millennium. As they grow in understanding and wisdom, perhaps they will remember the mysterious and wondrous world of "Light,"

Table of Contents

The Strange Door

Olivia had just turned ten years old, and was the oldest child in her family of five. This was the reason she was allowed to attend her grandmother's funeral. Wearing a yellow polka-dotted summer dress, she looked pretty with her long blonde hair and big blue eyes. She sat quietly beside her mother inside the old ivy-covered church. Olivia was rather tired after the long trip from the United States to the small village of Amesbury nestled in the English countryside. She watched as people filed past the coffin covered with white lilies. The sweet-smelling fragrance from the flowers wafted through the old stone church as the organ resonated with the hymn, "Going Home." Sunlight filtered through stained glass windows, casting blue and rosy-pink colors on the white silk lining of the casket. Sitting in the hand-carved wooden pew, thoughts of her last visit with Grandmother four years ago poured into her mind...

Grandmother had been a small woman with bright blue eyes, and a mound of white hair that looked like a pile of whipped cream swirled on top of her head. She smiled when she spoke, showing a dimple on each cheek. Olivia had sat on her grandmother's lap in the rocking chair as Grandmother spoke to her.

"Close your eyes, Olivia, and think of the most beautiful place you can imagine. Imagine yourself there." Olivia's thoughts were of a circus: carousels, eating cotton candy, and sucking on lollipops. As Olivia rocked on her grandmother's lap, she had thought of the most delightful things she could imagine before closing her eyes and falling asleep.

When the last person had passed the casket, her mother stood up, startling Olivia back into the present time. Feeling unsure of what to expect, she walked quietly beside her mother while holding tightly onto her hand. As they stood by the casket, she watched her mother quietly sobbing and dabbing her tears with a white lace handkerchief. Lying there in the casket, her grandmother looked exactly as Olivia had remembered. It appeared as if she had just laid down on a silky white pillow for an afternoon nap. She even had a slight smile on her lips, with the faintest show of a dimple on each cheek.

Soon, everyone began to leave the pews and follow the pall-bearers down the steps to the back of the church, to the grave-yard. There, people gathered to hear final prayers and say their "good-byes" with hugs to family members.

It began to mist as Olivia and her mother left the graveyard and walked a short distance down the wet cobblestone street in front of the church to the cottage where Grandmother had lived. Mother wanted to revisit her childhood home where she played in the garden and rode her bicycle on the paths in the village. She also wanted to choose a few special family heirlooms to send back to the United States. The antique dealers were scheduled to come tomorrow morning to take away the remaining items.

Within minutes they arrived at a quaint brown-stone storybook cottage. While Mother stopped to search her bag for the house keys, Olivia opened the gate and skipped ahead to peek in the window. On the window ledge were wooden flower boxes overflowing with pink and white petunias. As Olivia approached, an old ginger-colored cat jumped from behind the flower boxes and disappeared into the garden. Mother unlocked the front door and Olivia hurried inside.

The house smelled of spices and lavender. The burgundy sofa, soft and inviting, was in the parlor with white crocheted doilies draped on the back and arms. A large bookcase filled with colorful leather bound books lined the wall. In the dining room, an oval oak table with a white lace tablecloth and chairs was centered in the room. Along the wall stood a china cupboard adorned with lovely blue and white plates. Mother stood in the doorway, taking a mental inventory of the rooms. Olivia noticed the stairway leading up to the bedroom.

"Oh, Mother, can I go upstairs and see if Grandmother's bedroom is the same?!" Olivia called out as she was already on her way up the stairs.

Her mother couldn't help but smile. "Yes, go right ahead."

Entering the bedroom, Olivia looked around and saw a brass bed, covered with a white bedspread embroidered with pink roses. A dark oval braided rug covered most of the floor. On the round table beside her bed was a Victorian lamp with pink roses painted on the white glass shade, and several photos in oval Florentine frames. Just as she remembered, the rocking chair was still there with Grandmother's knitting bag next to it.

She glanced around the room at the old familiar things. An old travel trunk with brass fittings, and a fringed black shawl draped over one end sat in the corner. Approaching the trunk, Olivia saw a door off to the side; an old carved wooden door leaning against the wall with a rusty key protruding from the keyhole. It was a most unusual door, a door unlike any she had ever seen. The wood was dark and rough, and engraved with unusual designs. Olivia moved closer to it. There were serpent-like wavy lines along with a moon and star carved into the door. Strangest of all, just below eye level, was a round, clear crystal embedded in the center of the door.

What an odd thing to see in a bedroom, Olivia thought.

Just then, Mother entered the room and sat down in the rocking chair to rest.

"Mother, come look at this old door! Why would Grandmother have a door like this in her bedroom?"

Mother stood up and walked over to the door, looking curiously at it. A faint smile appeared on her lips as she traced the outline of the carved designs with her fingertips.

"Come sit with me in the rocking chair, and I will tell you the story about this door. The story your grandmother told to me when I was your age." Mother sat down in the chair again. Olivia, eager to hear the story, squeezed in beside her mother and snuggled in close.

Many years ago, when your grandmother, Grace, was about your age, she had a twin brother named David. The twins were totally opposite from one another. Grandmother Grace had blonde hair, blue eyes, and a happy disposition. David had dark hair and eyes, and was inclined to be mischievous. He delighted in teasing and playing tricks on his sister. They lived in a large manor house in the English countryside. Behind the manor house was a garden surrounded by a high stone wall. The wall was covered with climbing roses and ivy. Lilac bushes and red bud trees were planted, concealing most of the wall.

After lunch one sunny afternoon, David and his sister went into the garden to play a game of croquet. While they were taking turns hitting the ball, David, being mischievous, decided to hit the ball as hard as he could. It rolled across to the far side of the garden under a huge tangle of climbing rose bushes. Grandmother was very annoyed as she ran after it. When she reached the climbing roses, she got down on her hands and knees to see exactly where the ball had gone. All she could see were leaves, branches, and tangled vines...

It must be way back there against the wall, she thought. As she crawled on her stomach searching for the ball, she noticed the edge of a wooden door. Quickly backing out from under the bushes, she stood up and waved to her brother. "David! Come here, quickly!" she yelled.

David dropped his croquet mallet and ran to see what she had found. Both crouching down on their hands and knees, they crawled under the bushes. Grandmother showed him the edge of the door.

"Why do you think this door is here?" she asked.

"I don't know, but let's try to open it. Run to the tool shed and bring back the hedge clippers and a screwdriver," David instructed excitedly.

Crawling back out into the garden, Grandmother ran as fast as she could to the tool shed. Soon, she returned, and they began to clip and pull away some of the brambles. David was still on his knees when he noticed the rusty key in the lock. He tried to turn the key with his fingers, but the lock was also rusted and stuck tight. The key would not budge.

"Here, let me put this screwdriver through the hole in the top of the key and see if I can turn it," said Grandmother as her brother moved out of the way. Sure enough, with one hard twist, the key turned the lock. The door gave a little jerk away from the wall, and David was able to push the door open farther.

" Here, climb under the bushes and let's see what's on the other side of the door." David helped his sister crawl under the hanging vines and thorny rose branches.

When both were on the other side of the door, they found themselves engulfed in dead silence, surrounded by a swirling gray mist with eerie dark shadows of trees and rocks appearing and disappearing before their eyes. The two children were ready to turn around and quickly crawl back through the door when Grandmother noticed a light coming from what appeared to be a tunnel. It glowed with a bluish hue, diminishing into a rose-pink color toward the center.

"Look, David! Let's see what's over there!" Grandmother exclaimed as she walked faster and faster toward the rosy light.

David followed. The light became brighter and turned into golden sunlight as they walked through the tunnel and emerged onto the most beautiful meadow they had ever seen. Walking hand in hand through a meadow of vibrant green grass, they saw brilliantly colored butterflies dipping and swirling among flowers radiating all the colors of the rainbow. Ladybugs and iridescent green beetles climbed blades of grass.

"Oh, David! I must pick a bouquet of these beautiful flowers for Mum!"

David sat down in the grass, twirling a stalk of bluebells between his fingers. He noticed that each time he picked a flower, another immediately grew back in its place. As Grandmother gathered daisies and bluebells, David sat watching each flower replace itself.

"This is a strange, strange place," David said. "Look how each flower reappears. What is this place?"

"I really can't say, but it is so lovely," Grandmother said as she adjusted the bouquet in the crook of her arm. With nothing to do, David decided to be impish and tease his sister.

"Look out! A snake!"

Just as he said it, he looked down and saw a big black snake slithering towards his feet. "Run!" he screamed as he grabbed his sister by the arm and ran toward the tall trees at the edge of the meadow. Finally, David stopped to catch his breath.

"Wow, that was close! Did you see that snake?!" David panted.

"I didn't see a thing," Grandmother answered as she calmly sat down under a tree to catch her breath. She had dropped most of the flowers she had picked.

"Well, I saw it," David snapped, "and it scared me to death. We're lucky to be alive!"

Grandmother, ignoring her brother's comment, looked at the remainder of the flowers in her hand and began to sort them into little bunches on the grass.

"I think you were just trying to scare me. Great... Now I've lost most of Mum's flowers. I think I'll make a daisy chain necklace to wear, and a crown for you out of these flowers. You can be my prince," she giggled as she began tying the stems of the flowers together.

David leaned against the tree trunk while watching his sister. It annoyed him that she seemed to be so calm and serene after what he considered a very frightening experience. He began to think of a way to *really* frighten her. He wanted to get even with her for making him feel foolish. *Perhaps a huge black bear coming out of the woods would be really scary*, thought David. *A big black bear snarling... with huge teeth and claws... That would do the trick.*

Looking away from her daisy chain, Grandmother screamed. "Run, David! A big black bear is coming toward us!" Jumping to her feet, she grabbed David by the hand, and they ran deeper and deeper into the woods as fast as they could. The pounding of the bear's huge paws and the snapping of twigs and branches as it bore down on them was absolutely terrifying. Grandmother managed to scream even as she gasped for breath.

Just then, David saw a narrow opening in an old oak tree that had rotted from the inside out. The opening was just large enough for both of them to squeeze through. David yelled, "Quick, duck in there!"

They were barely able to squeeze through just as the bear approached the entrance. Growling and clawing, it attempted to enter after them. The twins clung to each other in fear, hoping the bear could not reach them.

Frightened, Grandmother covered her eyes with her hands and cried, "Somebody, please, help us!"

Suddenly, all became quiet and still. The bear vanished and in its place appeared a white shimmering light.

"Wow…" David whispered. "Look, look how bright."

Grandmother slowly lowered her hands and saw the light shimmering in sort of a blue and pink hue. It seemed welcoming and warm. "Let's peek out and see what it is."

The light had a calming effect on the children as they edged toward the opening. It grew bigger and brighter. There in the midst of the trees, a body of light was forming. Soon, the most beautiful "being" they had ever seen appeared and stood before them. It seemed to be almost transparent, yet the children were able to see what appeared to be a human form.

After they crawled out of the opening, the children asked at the same time, "Who are you?"   "My name is Light," the being answered. The melodic feminine voice was warm and reassuring.

"H-how did you know we were here?" David stammered.

"I heard you call for help," Light answered.

"We were so scared," said Grandmother. "We didn't know what to do. Where is this place?" she asked, feeling more at ease.

"This is the *Realm of Dreams Come True*. Anything you say or think will immediately come true."

"Oh... So that's why we saw the bear and the snake," David muttered.

'"Yes, and we must always be very careful what we think and say here because it will immediately materialize. Come, I will show you what I mean," she said as she turned to lead the way. Light walked along a path through the trees, and the children followed her in silence. They walked for some time until they reached the edge of the forest.

"Look," Light said, stopping suddenly.

In the distance, shimmering in the sunlight, stood a great castle made of pure crystal, emitting colors of the rainbow. Light pointed toward the castle.

"There is where your dreams on Earth come true."

Walking toward the castle, David and his sister could not take their eyes from it. They had never seen anything so big and beautiful. The tall towers topped with turrets glistened in the sunlight and the golden doors gleamed with radiant beauty. Light, David, and Grandmother walked up the steps through huge golden doors that opened into a long hall.

As they entered, the children noticed the walls were covered with pictures of every shape and size one could imagine. There were square, round, rectangular, and oval ones. Others hung from the ceiling like Christmas ornaments, and there were others attached to thin poles along the wall. Some of the pictures were of splendid buildings surrounded by parks with merry-go-rounds. A few were of people like scientists, school teachers, nurses, and doctors. Each one of the pictures was different. Some were extraordinarily beautiful with loving families and peaceful landscapes, while others were horrifyingly ugly with wars and other horrific deeds. In two of the pictures, they recognized themselves. One of Grandmother teaching school, and another of David exploring in the jungles and forests for plant specimens.

"Light, could you please tell us what these pictures mean?" David asked.

"I will explain to you, my dear ones. On Earth, a mortal's thoughts begin to create pictures with very faint etchings here in the *Realm of Dreams Come True*. Each thought and word adds more detail to the picture until it eventually becomes complete in fine detail. Over time, the picture is ready to become real. When a mortal truly wants his dream to be real with all of his heart, his deep feelings are transferred to this realm. The picture, once a dream, now becomes the life of the mortal."

Light pointed to a picture showing Grandmother teaching little children at school.

"Just as you play school with your dolls, you will become a teacher if you believe it already to be true," Light explained. "As you can see, even the ugly pictures of wars and crimes are created by people's hate and powerful feelings of injustice toward one another."

David and his sister were astounded at all of the incredible things Light told them about the pictures in the *Realm of Dreams Come True*. Realizing they had been away from home longer than usual, the children grew concerned their mother would be worried.

"It's late," Grandmother spoke up. "We must go home."

"But how can we find our way?" David asked, shrugging his shoulders.

"Oh, do not fear, my little ones. I will take you there. Please remember the things you saw and heard while you were here. Few mortals ever come to this realm."

Light led them away from the castle, took them back through the forest to the edge of the meadow, and through the light tunnel and mist until they were back at the door in the garden wall. The children hugged Light and said good-bye, and assured her that they would never forget her...ever.

As they crawled out from under the dried brambles back into their garden, they noticed how unkempt and overgrown it had become. The lawn chairs and benches seemed to be in need of paint and repair. The steps to the kitchen were broken and the door was hanging crooked on its hinges.

David and his sister ran into the house, calling to their mother. They found a gray-haired woman who held her hands to her face in disbelief. She held her arms out to the two young children and hugged them tenderly. Although she appeared much older and thinner than they remembered, David and his sister recognized their mother. As they embraced, their mother said her prayers had been answered. The children asked what had happened, and why everything had changed. They had been gone for such a short time.

Mother told them how everyone thought they had been kidnapped from the garden and taken away. Their father had gone to fight in the terrible war and never returned. Her life had been sad and lonely living without her family.

The children told their mother about the door in the garden wall, and how behind the door was an enchanted place. How they met Light, who was like an angel, a shimmering "spiritual being" and the castle in *The Realm of Dreams Come True*. They thought they had been gone only a short time, but when they returned, everything had changed. While hugging them tightly, their mother listened with tears in her eyes to their stories, smiled, and told them again how happy she was they had finally returned.

While they were in the realm, many years had passed. The children's friends had grown up and married. Some of them had left the village while others had stayed. Whenever the unusual story about David and his sister was mentioned, people would quickly change the subject and talk about other things. The children never again spoke about the door in the garden wall, and over the years, the story was forgotten.

David grew up and became a scientist. He married and moved away to Cambridge, England. Grandmother became a school teacher and lived with her mother. After her mother died, Grandmother met and married a wonderful man. She gave birth to a daughter who they named Lucia, meaning "light." Years later, after Grandmother's husband died, she sold the old manor house and moved to a smaller house in the village.

One day, she read in the local newspaper that a wealthy man bought the old manor house and was planning to turn it into an English Country Inn. The renovations had already begun, and the article mentioned that a parking lot was to be where the garden was located. Grandmother laid down the newspaper, placed her black shawl around her shoulders, and rode her bicycle to the manor house in the country.

Bulldozers were already at work clearing the garden and knocking down the garden walls. Grandmother got off of her bicycle and hurried to the garden where piles of rubble had been pushed into large heaps. She saw, on top of a large pile of stones and rose brambles, the old wooden door with the key still hanging from the keyhole.

Grandmother walked up to the man who was issuing orders to the workmen.

"Kind sir," she said gesturing toward the old house, "this was my family home. I was born and raised here, and I also raised my family here. I would like to make a request of you."

"And what would that be?" the man answered in a rather gruff voice, though he seemed somewhat curious.

"I would like one of your men to take that old door over there on that pile of rubble to my house in the village. I will pay whatever you ask for your trouble."

The foreman looked at the door. His face softened into a grin as he turned toward Grandmother "Yes, ma'am. I'll have a couple of my men do it this very afternoon. Where do you live?"

When Mother had finished talking, Olivia, thinking about the story, sat looking at the old door standing against the bedroom wall. It had been a fascinating story indeed.

"Well, Olivia, I must go downstairs and finish selecting the things we want to have shipped home with us," Mother said as she moved Olivia aside and stood to leave. "It will only take a few moments, so please come along quickly."

"I will," Olivia replied, walking over to the old door. Once again, she ran her fingers over the carvings in the wood, then bent over to look into the round crystal embedded in the door. Peering into the crystal, she saw a pale blue and pink light. When she looked deep into the light, she saw a green meadow with beautiful flowers. There, she saw a little girl with blonde hair and a little boy with dark hair. They were holding hands, laughing, and running though the meadow.

"Olivia? Olivia! What is taking you so long?!" Mother called from downstairs. "Please come downstairs right away!"

Startled by her mother's voice, Olivia turned away from the door and called back, "I'm coming now!"

As she passed her grandmother's bed, she noticed a photo on the nightstand. It was of a little blonde-haired girl and a little dark-haired boy in a green meadow full of flowers. Olivia stopped and stared at the photograph. She realized these were the same children she had just seen in the crystal!

She stepped out of the bedroom. Holding onto the hand railing, Olivia slowly walked down the stairs thinking about what she had just seen. Her mother was standing by the front door, placing her hat on and buttoning her jacket.

"We must leave now. It is getting dark, and tomorrow we have to return early. The packers will be here to remove what we want to take with us, and we'll leave the rest here for the antique dealers." Her mother opened the door, then locked it behind them. Walking down the steps, Olivia looked back once again at her grandmother's house. They strolled out of the gate and turned to go down the cobblestone street.

Gazing up at her mother, Olivia pleaded, "Mother, may we *please* take the old door with us?"

The Crystal Cage

$\mathcal{Y}$ears had passed since Olivia acquired the door from her grandmother's bedroom in England. She had grown up, married, and moved to the countryside in upstate New York. Olivia and her husband had found and bought a house they loved. It was an old stone Tudor-style house with tiny glasspane windows and a gabled roof. Behind the house they created a colorful flower garden, and enclosed it with a high, native stone wall. At the farthest end of the garden, near the trailing ivy and climbing roses, they had fitted into the wall the old carved door with the key still intact.

Not long after Olivia and her husband had settled into their new home, they became proud parents of fraternal twins: a girl and a boy. The little girl with big blue eyes and curly blonde hair was named Hannah Joy, and the little boy with big brown eyes and straight hair was named Noah Paul. They were a very happy family.

Soon after the children were born, Olivia had the gardener plant a lilac bush in front of the old door. She remembered the story about her grandmother and her brother who went through the door in the garden. When they returned, it was a time far into the future where they had remained children, but their mother and friends had grown much older. The thought of her own children getting caught in such a time warp seemed awfully silly, but was too frightening for Olivia to take any chances. As time passed, the lilac bush grew big and strong until it covered the door completely.

When the children became older, fearing they may one day discover the door on their own, Olivia told them the story her mother had told her. She warned them, "Never open the door and go through to the other side. For if you do, when you return, everything will have changed. You will remain children while everyone else will have aged."

Time passed, and while the children usually got along quite well, they were as opposite as night and day as they grew into their own individual personalities. Hannah was bright, lively, and loved to play with other children. She always had an activity going on where she needed a playmate. Hannah especially loved to pretend she was a dancer or an actress on stage, playing dress-up in her mother's old clothes.

Noah, on the other hand, was more pensive and rather fond of nature. He loved looking at his natural history books and exploring outside. He grew plants in glass jars, collected rocks and shells, and had an aquarium and an ant farm. He enjoyed drawing and sculpting insects, plants, and birds. He also had a deep desire to understand how nature was connected, and how it worked in harmony.

One warm, quiet afternoon during summer vacation, Noah was sitting in his bedroom contemplating the complexity of butterflies. He had found a cocoon and watched as a blue swallow-tail butterfly emerged from the chrysalis. Never had he been so in awe or inspired by anything that wonderful in nature. Noah decided to sculpt a butterfly out of clay. Sitting at the table in his bedroom, he formed the clay into a butterfly. He was putting on the final details when in bounded Hannah, announcing she needed him right that instant to play a game of Monopoly with her! Noah, who was usually accommodating to his sister's intrusions, emphatically told her, "No!" since he was in the middle of his own project.

That, unfortunately, did not sit well with Hannah. Being more than a bit miffed at her brother's answer, Hannah walked right up to the table, and with one slam of her fist, smashed the clay sculpture into the wax paper.

"There! Now you don't have a project!" she exclaimed with a giggle, then ran to her room and slammed the door shut.

Noah was furious! He wanted to cry, but knew he didn't dare because that would really make Hannah's day. He sat with his head in his hands, trying to control his urge to break down his sister's door and have it out with her. Instead, he scraped the clay off the paper and formed it into a round ball. Rolling the ball of clay around in the palm of his hand, he decided to go downstairs and tell his mom what Hannah had done.

Calling to his mom, he entered the kitchen and found her talking on the telephone. She was too engaged in conversation with a friend to pay attention to him. Noah stood looking at his mother while holding the clay out to her as he tried to mouth the words of what happened upstairs. She covered the phone and asked him to wait until she was finished, then waved him away with her hand.

Feeling dejected, Noah walked out of the kitchen to the far end of the garden, crawled under the large lilac bush, and began to pout. He sat there wiping tears from his eyes. Angrily, he threw the clay into the lilac bush. When the clay hit the branches, he saw something move and take flight. It was a butterfly; the largest, most beautiful butterfly he had ever seen.

It's as large as my hand! Noah thought as he scrambled to his knees and parted the branches to get a better look as the butterfly fluttered away. Its wings glittered like white opals, with blue and yellow dots on its lower wings. It seemed to glint and sparkle as it flew over the garden wall. Noah had never seen anything like it in any of his nature books before, and he just knew he had to chase after it for a better look. This was surely one of nature's wonders!

In order not to lose sight of the butterfly, he needed to get quickly to the other side of the wall. Looking around, Noah realized he was sitting in front of the old door. While on his knees, he frantically reached for the rusted key in the lock. He turned it as hard as he could, but it wouldn't budge. Picking up a piece of a broken branch that was on the ground by his foot, he stuck it through the hole at the top of the key and gave it a hard twist. The key clicked, and the door gave a little jolt away from the wall.

Noah hurriedly pulled and cleared away some of the vines and branches covering the door. Now, he was able to get his hands between the door and the wall. Pushing with all of his might, he could only open the door just a few inches; just enough so that he could barely squeeze his body through to the other side.

Standing up, he found himself in a gray mist that seemed to swirl around his feet and body. Noah began to feel frightened and was ready to turn around and go back when off in the distance, he caught a glimpse of the butterfly. In the haze, trying not to lose sight of it, he raced after it. Soon, the mist began to lift and Noah could see what appeared to be a tunnel of bluish light in front of him.

Chasing after the butterfly, Noah followed it through the tunnel into a meadow that dazzled with brilliant emerald green grass and jewel-colored flowers. The butterfly would land on a flower every now and then, just long enough for Noah to almost catch up to it before it flew a little farther away to land again. Noah chased after it farther and farther across the meadow until he came to a wooded area where large oak trees grew with out-stretched branches reaching up to a cloudless sky.

The butterfly flitted on through the trees with Noah in pursuit until they came to the edge of a clear lake glistening in the sunshine. On the trunk of an old oak tree, the butterfly rested. The butterfly began to glow as Noah inched closer. It became larger and brighter, like a Fourth of July sparkler. Noah stopped in his tracks. He didn't move as he watched the strange metamorphosis take place. Soon, standing in front of him was a beautiful being almost like a transparent shadow, yet having a form like an angel.

"Who... are you?" Noah stammered, trying to catch his breath from running.

"My name is Light," the being said in a calm melodic voice.

"Where... am I?"

"This is *The Realm of Being,* where humans learn to become *true* human beings."

"I... I don't understand," Noah stuttered, still feeling a little afraid.

"Don't be fearful. I won't harm you." She held her hand out to Noah. "Come with me and I will show you what I mean."

By this time, Noah was feeling more relaxed and willing to go with her. Talking her hand, they walked together to the edge of the lake.

"There." Light pointed into the water. "Look very closely into the bubbles along the water's edge."

Noah looked, and then looked again. Hundreds, maybe thousands of bubbles were floating to the top of the water: along the edges, around the water lilies, everywhere.

"But what am I to see?"

"Look deep within each bubble, and tell me what you see."

Noah crouched down and put his face as close as he could to the water. He even got on his hands and knees, and put his face still closer to the bubbles. Within each bubble there appeared to be a person, a human being in a miniature environment. An environment uniquely different, yet similar to the others.

"Light, I can barely make out what I am seeing here. It seems as though there is a human in each bubble, like a... a crystal cage."

Light smiled. "Hold still. I will make you smaller so you can see more clearly into the 'crystal cage.'"

As she raised her hands over Noah, little sparkles of light drifted down over him, and the two of them became smaller and smaller until they were small enough to fit inside the bubble. When Noah looked into the crystal orbs, he was able to see and understand each person's individual perception of their own world. Some bubbles were colorful and exciting, some were lifeless and drab, while others were busy with animation and activity, yet none of them seemed to be aware of the other's existence. Although the humans thought they were together, they were unable to see the transparent walls that separated them from the other. They were able to share their ideas, thoughts, and feelings, but in reality, the crystal cage of their own mind kept them separated by transparent walls; walls they could not see.

As Noah and Light were looking into the bubbles, Light explained that it was very difficult for one to enter another; however, she would allow Noah to enter a few of them so that he could truly understand the meaning of the "crystal cage."

Light touched the side of one of the bubbles, and an opening appeared for Noah to slip through. "I will wave to you when you are to come out of the bubble. Be sure to leave immediately," she warned sternly. "If you stay longer and do not return immediately, you will become trapped in their crystal cage."

Noah agreed as he stepped through the opening of the bubble. In the center of the bubble stood a young boy. He was an only child, being raised by his mother. She worked and was not able to spend much time with him. He longed for a dad like other boys or someone older to pal around and play with him. Instead, he watched a lot of television, ate snacks, and tried to finish his homework. This boy was unaware that Noah was with him.

Noah began to walk toward the boy when he saw Light waving frantically for him to come out. He remembered Light's stern words to return immediately when she waved to him. Instead, Noah hesitated, wanting to spend a moment longer. Light reached in and pulled him through the bubble wall.

"That was a close one!" Light exclaimed. "I have other bubbles for you to enter before I can explain to you how people become *true* human beings. How did you feel in there?"

"It felt so strange to experience what goes on inside a person's mind. To be able to think what they are thinking, and to feel what they are feeling!"

"Come, I have another crystal cage for you to enter. You may be very surprised by this one." She smiled, showing him a bubble with a little blonde-haired girl skipping rope.

"Ugh, Light, that is Hannah in there!" Noah groaned. "Do you want me to go into *her* bubble?"

"Why not?" Light asked as she held the opening for Noah to enter. "Now, be sure to come out when I wave to you, and don't hesitate this time. I don't want you to be trapped in her cage."

When Noah stepped in, he began to feel much lighter and brighter, filled with joy and spontaneity. He felt himself attracted to people in a way he had never experienced before. He wanted to play, talk, and discuss ideas about what was happening in each person's life. He heard music as though for the first time as it resounded through his body. He enjoyed telling jokes and making people laugh. He was aware of the feelings between Hannah and her mother, the closeness they felt for one another. He also realized why she wanted to tease him when he wouldn't pay attention to her. Now, he understood her attachment to her twin brother; how much she loved and depended on him as her true friend. Noah was feeling happy and sad at the same time. He wanted to go to her and tell her how sorry he was for not considering her feelings. He wanted to give her a hug.

Again, he saw Light waving frantically, motioning for him to come out. Her face was contorted and her mouth was forming a loud, "Now!" This made Noah stop and remember Light telling him not to hesitate for an instant, but to come out immediately. He turned around and, again, Light pulled him through the opening of the bubble just as it was closing. In a very stern manner, Light explained again how important it was not to hesitate. To hesitate meant to be trapped in that human's thoughts and feelings forever, and never to be able to escape.

"Now, do you understand how important it is for you to obey my exact words?" Light asked.

"Yes, ma'am. I... I just wanted to tell her something," Noah mumbled, feeling rather embarrassed at being scolded.

"Noah, if you *promise* to obey my signal, I will give you one more very special experience. You must give your word of honor that you will leave as soon as I signal. You need at least three experiences in order to understand how people become *true* human beings."

Noah did not know whether or not he was up to another scolding or if he even wanted another experience. He stood looking into the water, and then at Light. With hesitation, he decided to go for it. *This time,* he would make sure, no matter what, to immediately leave the bubble.

"Okay, I want to do it."

"Good for you! Let's go over to the far side of the lake. That side is special."

This time, looking into the bubbles, Noah could see animals of many different kinds: dogs, cats, horses, cows, tigers, and more.

"Oh! Do you mean I will feel what they are feeling?" Noah asked.

"Yes, and you will be very surprised," Light answered as she opened the side of the bubble where a young dog was sitting by the side of the road.

When Noah entered, he immediately began to feel lost and bewildered, then confused and agitated. He was able to experience himself as an adorable puppy. Children were giggling and playing with him, giving him treats, and hugging him. The dog romped, played, and slept at the foot of their bed. When the children grew older, and the dog grew older, they no longer wanted to play with him. They yelled at him when he barked to get their attention. They made him sleep outside in a cold doghouse. Sometimes, when he tried to follow because he wanted to be with them, he was chained to the fence.

One day, the family went for a drive and their dog was allowed to go along. Oh, how contented and peaceful it all seemed with everyone talking and stroking his head... all except for the little girl who sat still in the back seat, tears filling her eyes and not saying a word. The car stopped, and everyone got out to enjoy a picnic and games. The dog loved playing "fetch the stick." He ran, jumped, and returned it each time the boy threw the stick. Then there was a long throw... a very long throw.

When the dog returned, the car was gone, the family was gone, and he was alone, waiting... waiting for his family to return. Still holding the stick in his mouth, looking at each passing car, he waited. After a very long time he began to run in circles, trying to catch the scent of the car tires.

Noah saw Light wave to him, and without hesitation he returned through the opening of the bubble. He felt a big knot in his throat, and tears welled up in his eyes.

"I feel terrible! Now, I understand. Even though an animal has no language, it does not mean that they are not aware of the bond they have with humans."

"Yes, Noah. Each new understanding creates an awareness in a human being. Sometimes we think we know and understand another person, but until we are able to feel what they feel or think the thoughts they think, we only can guess their thoughts and feelings."

"Is there a way we can ever truly understand and become a *true* human being?" Noah asked.

Light pointed toward the water.

"As you can see, the bubbles in the lake contain all living life forms. They are constantly rising and sinking, moving to one side, and then to the other, connecting with other bubbles, then splitting apart. On a seemingly endless journey, they are trying to be a part of one another, yet as each human gains new information and experiences, he grows in love and compassion. Only then will he be able to enter another's crystal cage. The cage will become larger and larger, filled with peace and harmony.

"You see, Noah, the Creator's plan of peace and harmony will return when we are able to connect our lives and form a giant sphere of love. This sphere will be filled with *true* human beings. They will know that the secret passageway to another bubble is through their own hearts, filled with love and compassion. All living entities have been created from the love of the Creator."

"Light? Do you think we will ever be able to live in peace and harmony in one big biosphere bubble?" Noah asked in wonder.

"Yes, my dear. All lines in a circle eventually meet. Perhaps you will be able to help others connect their bubbles, or 'crystal cages,' as you call them." Light smiled and raised her hands. Glittering sprinkles of light fluttered over Noah, and he returned to his true size.

"Oh, it must be late!" Noah exclaimed anxiously. "Mom will be worried. I'd better return to the garden. How can I return? I don't remember the way."

"Do not be concerned. I will take you back. Remember, I was the one who brought you here," said Light, smiling and waving her arms like a butterfly.

When the two of them approached the door in the garden wall, Noah covered his face with his hands.

"Oh, no! Oh, no! Now I remember what my mother told me! She said to never, ever go through this door, because when you return, everything will be changed to a future time. Everything will be old," moaned Noah. "Oh, Light, help me! I'm afraid! What shall I do?!"

"Do not be afraid. I will tell you how to return so that everything will be the same as you left it. You must listen carefully and do exactly as I say."

"I will!" Noah promised.

"After you slip through the door, you will have only a very short time to do what I am going to tell you. Count like this: crystal one, crystal two, crystal three, and keep counting. You must complete the instructions I am about to give you before you reach crystal sixty."

Noah was very tense, and was trying so hard to hear each step of the instructions and remember them.

Light continued, "When you slip through the door into the garden, find the crystal in the center of the door, then turn it three times to the left and once to the right. Then with your fingers, pull it out of the door. If you are able to pull the crystal out of the door, all will be the same as you left it. If you are not successful in getting the crystal out, all will have changed before your eyes. Now, repeat the instructions to me."

Noah repeated them perfectly, then tried to squeeze his body through the narrow opening from the door.

"Good luck, Noah. Remember all that you saw and heard here." Light touched Noah's cheek with her hand. "I will never forget you."

"And I will never forget you, Light. Thank you, thank you for everything!" Noah called over his shoulder as he slipped through to the other side of the wall.

Finding himself on his knees among the lilac branches, Noah reached for the crystal and began to count. "Crystal one, crystal, two..."

Noah continued counting and turning while trying to push away the leaves and branches covering the door. It was difficult keeping the branches from swinging back into his face and covering the crystal.

"Crystal thirty, crystal thirty-one..." As he tried to turn the crystal three times to the left, Noah's fingers kept slipping because of the sweat on his hands. He couldn't seem to get a good grip on it.

"Crystal thirty-nine, crystal forty..." Finally, Noah completed the three turns to the left and once to the right.

"Crystal forty-three, crystal forty-four..." *Now to pull it out of the door*, Noah thought. His fingers slipped from it again as he tried to grasp the crystal.

"Crystal fifty, crystal fifty-one..."

Noah was frantically trying to hold onto the crystal. He looked down at his feet and saw the stick he had used to turn the key in the keyhole. He grabbed the stick and broke one end sharp as he continued counting, "Crystal fifty-six, crystal fifty-seven..." Pushing the pointed end of the stick up under the edge of the crystal, Noah gave a hard jerk with both hands as he said, "Crystal fifty-nine..." Out flew the crystal from the old door and rolled onto the ground just as he counted, "Crystal sixty." Noah held his breath and turned around, not knowing what to expect.

"Noah? Noah, where *are* you?!" yelled Hannah at the top of her lungs. "I know you're hiding from me, and I am going to find you!"

She turned around and went back to the house, stomped up the steps, opened the door to the kitchen, and went into the house.

Noah couldn't believe how wonderful it was to hear Hannah's voice again, and to see the house and garden just the way they always were! Noah picked up the crystal and put it into his pocket. He parted the lilac branches, and walked across the garden to the house.

"Here I am, Hannah!" Noah yelled as he ambled toward the kitchen door. "What do you want?!"

Hannah stuck her head out of the kitchen window and, in her sweetest voice, said, "Noah, will you play a game with me? I've made up a very special game all about butterflies." She smiled at her brother, then giggled.

The Door of Symbols

*T*en years passed...

The afternoon was hot and muggy. Slipping off his shoes and loosening his tie and collar button, Noah lay on his bed and stared at the ceiling. He was tired from the long trip he had taken from England to his home in upstate New York. He had returned prematurely from school to attend his grandmother's funeral. All of the people who came to pay their respects and comfort his family had gone. It felt good just to lie there alone.

Noah had grown into a fine young man. He was into his second-year studies in natural science at the University of Cambridge, and would soon return to finish the year.

He began to think back to the time he went through the door in the garden wall. His grandmother was the one who had brought the old door to New York, and Noah's mom, Olivia, had placed it in her garden wall. He thought, *I wonder where that old door came from in the first place? And where is the crystal I pulled out of it all those years ago?*

Noah glanced around his bedroom. His mom had kept his room just the way he had left it. School memorabilia still hung on the walls and the desk and bookcase remained the same. Noah's eyes stopped when he saw the small wooden box on the very top shelf of his bookcase. Years ago, it was there in that box that he had placed the crystal from the door in the garden wall. He had never told anyone about his experience of entering the dimension of Light. First of all, he knew he would have been in serious trouble for disobeying his parents. Also, he felt certain no one would believe his incredible story.

Noah rolled over and looked out the bedroom window. He could see that the lilac bush had grown to fully cover the door in the garden wall. As a matter of fact, it was impossible to see any part of it. The vines and climbing roses had covered every inch of the wall.

"Noah? Noah! Come down and give me a hand with this thing!" It was Dad calling from downstairs.

"I'm coming!" shouted Noah as he got up and slipped on his shoes. Standing at the top of the stairs, he could see his father wet with perspiration and wiping his brow with his handkerchief.

"What's up, dad?" he called out as he sauntered down the stairs.

"Your mom had me bring over a few things that she wanted to keep from your grandmother's house. There's a pretty heavy trunk out there in the pickup, and I could use a hand with it."

"Sure, I'll give you a hand."

Carrying the old trunk into the house, Dad called out toward the kitchen, "Olivia, where do you want this old trunk of your mother's?!"

"Just take it up to Noah's room for now, and I'll get to it later," she answered. "I want to get a good look at what's in it before we take it up to the attic."

The old black trunk with brass fittings was bulky and heavy as the two of them carried it carefully up the stairs to Noah's room. They heaved a sigh of relief when they set it down and stood back to take a better look at the family heirloom.

"What do you think, dad? Have any idea how old this trunk is or where it came from?" Noah asked as he examined the lock and the brass fittings along the sides and top of the trunk.

"I don't have any idea, son. You'll have to ask your mother about that. There are still a few more things to bring in. I could use a little help," he said as he left the room. Noah followed his father out the door and down the stairs. Hannah was waiting at the bottom when they came down. She was anxious to see Grandmother's treasures.

Hannah matured into a lovely young woman and studied at the Julliard School of Dance in New York City. She had arrived the previous day, and after a few days at home would return to school to finish out the year.

"Oh, Noah, what do you think is in that old trunk?" she asked excitedly. "Let's see what else dad brought from Grandmother's attic." She hurried out to the truck, not waiting for Noah to answer.

Noah and his dad carried the rest of the boxes and books into the house, then sat on the sofa to rest. Dad decided they had had enough work for the day, and anything else would just have to wait until tomorrow. Exhausted, Noah excused himself and went upstairs to his room to take a nap. Already tired from his long trip, he instantly fell into a deep sleep.

When he awoke, his bedside lamp was still on. The clock on the nightstand read 3:00 a.m. Noah lay on his bed, eyes wide open, staring at the old trunk in the corner of the room. Knowing he wasn't about to go back to sleep, he stood up and walked over to the trunk. Bending over it, he twisted the key in the rusty lock and heard the click and release. He removed the latches on both sides of the lock and slowly lifted the lid. A musty odor wafted out of the trunk and filled his nostrils. He took a deep

breath and held it while he opened the lid wider. A black crocheted shawl was spread on top. He lifted it, and underneath
he saw old books, photographs, and letters tied with a ribbon.

Quickly, he placed the shawl on the bed and took out the
books and photographs, examining each carefully. Near the
bottom of the trunk was a dark rectangular wooden box with
strange symbols engraved on it. Noah held it in his hands and
tried to determine how to open it. It seemed to be a puzzle
box, one of those that needed several different panels released
before the top would open. After several tries, the lid of the box
slid opened. Inside were pages of yellowed paper, one rolled
inside the other.

Why, these must be a hundred years old, Noah thought as he
carefully unrolled the outer scroll. Across the top of the paper
written with a quill in black ink was *The Door of Symbols.*

Noah's mouth dropped open, and his eyes widened in
disbelief.

"Could this be about the old door in the garden wall?" he
whispered to himself. His hands were shaking as he walked
toward the light from the lamp on his nightstand. Propping
himself with the pillow against the headboard of the bed, he
read the words written on the scroll.

Alexandria, Egypt
The year of our Lord 1887

I, Captain Jon Michael Ashcroft, being of sound mind and body, do write this epistle telling of the fateful happenings regarding the acquisition of the Door of Symbols. Each word I write is the truth of my experience and understanding , so help me God.

Signed,

Captain Jon Michael Ashcroft

In the year 1881, in the month of August, I was the captain of a vessel in Her Majesty's Royal Navy. My port of station during this time was in Alexandria, Egypt. We had been out to sea and were on our home voyage back to Alexandria. Sailing along the coast of North Africa, a severe storm broke out over the sea. The wind blew fiercely, and the waves lashed at the sides and up over the rails of our vessel until we feared for our very lives. The men were sorely vexed, and I prayed for our safe return to home port. All night the wind howled and the sea pitched our ship until weariness overtook us all.

At last, the dawn broke, and the sea became as still as a dead man's chest. I went below to my cabin and fell into a deep sleep. I have no idea how long I slept before I awoke, upon hearing a faint call for help. It sounded like a moaning coming from the starboard side of the vessel. I pulled on my boots, and went up on deck.

Looking over the side of the ship, I spied near the vessel a man floating on top of what appeared to be a wooden door. He was chained to it by one of his wrists and struggled to stay atop his makeshift raft. I called the master of arms over and instructed him and some of the crew to lower a rope ladder and sling over the side. By means of ropes and a pulley, they were able to lift the door and the man over the railing onto the deck. The poor soul was barely breathing and looked as though he was not long for this world. Only the Lord knows how or what had kept him alive through the storm.

Calling a crewman over with a hammer and chisel, I asked him to break the chain and lock fastened to the poor man's wrist. They then carried him to my quarters for proper care and rest. Having a good deal of knowledge in medical herbal stimulants for exhaustion and shock, I took it upon myself to nurse this poor soul back to health, leaving the brunt of his fate in the care of Divine Providence.

Days passed and only a glimmer of hope had I for this young man as he drifted in and out of consciousness. On the last day before docking in the port of Alexandria, I went below to take my evening meal. There, lo and behold, the young man was sitting up in bed holding the journal that I kept by his bedside. I was startled at first to see him awake and sitting up. Then a gladness came over me, and I shouted a loud, "Hello, my friend! And how might you be this evening?" as I rushed over to greet him with a warm handshake.

He smiled weakly and lifted his hand to greet me. In a heavy accent, he said, "My name is Kabir, and I am from India." He then asked how he happened to be here in a bed, and on what ship, and to where were we headed?

I answered his questions one after the other, and invited him to join me for a bite to eat. In his weakened condition, he was only able to eat a bit of bread sopped in a small portion of hearty beef broth and drink a swallow or two of ale. Before I knew it, he drifted off into a sound sleep, and I had to wait until the morrow to speak again with him.

I awoke early, dressed, and hurried topside. The boatswain was giving orders to the crew to lower the sails before entering port and docking. As soon as we docked, I instructed one of the crew to immediately take Kabir from below to my quarters in the city.

"What about the old door?" he asked, motioning to the wooden slab the young man had been chained to. That was the first time I had given it a good look. Walking over to it, I noticed the odd carvings and the crystal embedded in the center of the door. "Keep it," I called out to the crewman. "Take it along with the young fellow to my quarters."

The crewman, Kabir, and the door were the first to leave. Within the hour, the last of the crew had disembarked from the ship. With a hearty thirst, they were headed toward the nearest taverns in the port. Upon leaving the ship, I engaged a carriage to take me to my quarters in the city so I could rest and look in on Kabir.

The English held a small post on the outskirts of Alexandria where I rented a private house with the appropriate number of domestic servants. Upon arriving, the head servant came running up to my carriage and requested that I come in quickly, as my guest was taking a turn for the worse. I asked the servant to have a cup of hot stimulating tea brought to the room.

When I entered his bedroom, Kabir opened his eyes and smiled weakly. I approached and offered my hand, but he was unable to respond. Immediately, I called for the head servant to quickly send the houseboy for the aid of a doctor. The tea arrived and after sipping it, Kabir seemed to revive somewhat.

Soon, the doctor arrived to examine the young man. He listened to Kabir's heart and lungs.

"It doesn't look good. This lad has taken a lot of water into his lungs, and he is weakened by exhaustion and exposure," murmured the doctor. Opening his bag, the doctor pulled out a small glass bottle and handed it to me.

"Here is a tonic to give him strength, and see to it that he eats twice a day; rice or gruel with broth to strengthen his blood. He may or may not make it..." Thanking him for coming so promptly, I paid the doctor and showed him to the door.

Three days passed, and I found Kabir strong enough to sit up so he could be taken into the garden for fresh air. As I pushed his wheel chair through the garden, he told me that he was to sail to Alexandria with a secret mission only he and his contact knew about. I asked him if he could reveal the mission to me so I could help in some way.

Kabir was very quiet, and I could tell he was weighing in his mind the consequences of his decision.

"I have a question to ask you," he said.

"Yes, what is it?"

"The door... where is it?"

"Do you mean that slab of wood you were chained to?" I asked, rather perplexed.

"Yes, yes, that one," he answered anxiously.

"Why, it's over there," I said, gesturing towards the shed.

"Will you please take me there? I must see it for myself," he insisted.

I wheeled his chair to the shed and unlocked the door. The light was dim inside, and the room was hot and dusty. I wheeled his chair in.

"There it is." I pointed towards the corner.

"Take me closer. I want to see it up close."

As we approached, he reached out his hand to touch the door. His fingers traced over the symbols and his spirit seemed to quicken as he touched the crystal.

"What is it? What is so special about this door?" I wondered as I observed his strange behavior.

"I am feeling rather tired. Would you please take me back?" Kabir whispered as he pulled his lap robe up around his chest.

When we entered his room, I helped the young man into bed and covered him with a warm blanket. As I turned to leave the room, once again, I asked, "Kabir, if you would tell me about your mission, perhaps I can help."

Kabir looked straight ahead, his dark eyes piercing the silence. "I cannot," he answered before his eyes closed.

The following day, I was summoned to the young man's room. His eyes were glassy, and beads of sweat dotted his brow.

"Captain Ashcroft... I must talk to you... This is very important..." Kabir whispered as I neared his bed.

I sat on the chair next to him and dropped my ear close to his lips. Feeling responsible for the lad, I said, "Kabir, tell me, tell me what I can do to help."

His dark hair was matted to his head with perspiration and his breathing was labored as he began to tell me the most incredible story I have ever heard. As I write, I swear every word is his true story as I am able to remember it.

Kabir's Story

I come from a village in the north of India, near the Himalayas. The village is called Saharanpur. Many monasteries are there and pilgrims from all over India make the holy pilgrimage in order to become enlightened. One of the mountains is considered to be the most holy. Those who enter the monasteries enter for many reasons. Very few have chosen to return to their homes, and those who do return become the enlightened teacher in their village. They say they have obtained wisdom beyond understanding. As far as I know, no one has ever spoken of the mysteries in this holy mountain.

One day, in my village, an old man approached me and asked if I would be willing to go on an adventure inside the mountain. He would give me a large sum of money if I would go into the mountain and bring back evidence of enlightenment that was said to be there. The sum was more than my family had ever seen, and with it, I knew they would never have to work again. I also knew the sacredness of this mountain, and to disturb what is holy could bring grave consequences to me and my family.

I was not a religious young man; however, after several days of considering what to do, I decided to accept the money and go into the sacred mountain. The old man was to give me half of the money before I entered, and the other half upon returning with proof. The very day I entered the mountain, I regretted making such a bargain .

The entrance was a large chamber that became smaller leading into a corridor. As I walked along, the corridor became narrower. My lantern flickered from a breeze flowing through the tunnel. I have no idea how long or how far I walked, but I soon came to the end. There, the tunnel forked to the right and to the left. I began to feel uneasy and wanted to turn around.

A whistling sound through the tunnel penetrated my ears. This sound created a most inharmonious effect in my mind and body. It rang in my ears, and the high-pitched tone caused my head to ache and my heart to pound. I placed my lantern on the ground and covered my ears with my hands to try to shut out the dreadful noise, but it only became louder and louder. I began to turn around and around in circles. Then I ran, stumbling, trying to get out of the cave.

At last, I tripped and fell to the ground. I must have hit my head on a rock and lost consciousness. When I awoke, it was pitch black... the most absorbing darkness I could ever imagine. I had no idea how long I had lain there.

I was terrified and began to cry out in desperation. "Help! Someone, help me!" The fear was overpowering.

All of a sudden, before my eyes, I saw a bluish light with a rose-pink color appearing in the center. I got to my knees and then stood up, watching the light grow larger and larger. It appeared to be a tunnel. I walked towards it, then through it.

Immediately, I found myself in a beautiful valley, radiant in golden light, and a meadow of lush green grass with wildflowers everywhere. The colors were vibrant, and the meadow seemed to be from a fantasy world, a world of perfection and beauty. Nothing I had ever seen or could imagine compared to it. I began walking towards a grove of trees, wondering if there were any villages or people about. As I approached the grove, I called out, "Hello! Hello, is anyone here?!"

A bright light appeared and grew larger. I stopped. There, standing before me, was a beautiful spirit being. It appeared transparent; a slender body with pale golden hair falling over the shoulders, and wearing a long, flowing white gown. It emitted the appearance of form and light.

"*Who are you?*" *I asked, not sure what to expect.*

"*My name is Light.*"

"*Where am I, and why are you here?*" *I asked, still feeling uneasy.*

"*You are in The Realm of the Fifth Dimension, and I am a spirit being of the First Cause. This is the true realm of your being.*"

"*I don't understand. First, I was in the cave in darkness, and now I am here. How did I get here, and why am I here?*" *I asked, feeling confused. Light came toward me and reached out her hand.*

"*Come with me, and I will tell you what every human longs to know.*"

Following along beside her, we walked to a grassy area near a large tree where she motioned me to sit down. Light began to tell me a most incredible story, yet one I seemed to remember from the depths of my soul.

"*Do you see far yonder toward the mountain?*" *Light asked.* "*There is the door you came through. It is called the Door of Symbols. Those symbols represent the keys to awaken a human's heart. Each human has within his heart a door that, when opened, no man can close. When a human seeks his true path in life, this path leads him to The Realm of the Fifth Dimension.*

"This is the heavenly home he has sought since the beginning of time. This path begins in his heart chamber, and there he will find the door that only he can open. The highest consciousness knocks at the door of the heart, and his human consciousness desires to open it. The open door will lead him here, the realm of love, wisdom, and understanding. It is the realm you mortals call Heaven.

"This is the Garden of Eden, where all life began... where the first perfect cause was created. It has been waiting all these eons for mankind to return and claim it with his highest and purest thoughts. You are now sitting under the Tree of Life. Remember, Kabir, when you desire it with your whole being, your frequency will rise to this perfected state."

I sat staring at Light, not wanting to hear another word from her lips. All of this frightened me. Not having a spiritual upbringing, I found her words difficult to understand. I only wanted to leave that place, go back to the entrance of the cave, and get the rest of my money from that old man.

Standing to leave, I asked, "Light, how can I go back? How can I go back to the cave and to my home?"

"I will show you the way." She turned toward the mountain, and we crossed the meadow. Light pointed to the tunnel of bluish light.

"There is the Door of Symbols, the opening to the third dimension, the realm of mortals. When you return, I hope you will remember all you have seen and heard while you were here. Now, you must remember something very important. When you enter the tunnel, keep to the right. Always go to the right, and you will see the light to the opening of the cave."

I thanked Light before hurrying into the tunnel. I hadn't gone far when I realized I did not have the proof to bring back to the old man: I would not get the rest of the money he promised me. I looked around for something to take with me, but saw nothing. Then I remembered the Door of Symbols. If I could take the door, it would truly prove everything. I returned, lifted the door off its hinges, and carried it on my back. It was heavy, but I was strong from carrying many baskets of rocks to build houses in my village.

As I walked through the tunnel, the ringing began to pound in my ears, once more, and I began to feel dizzy. I was determined to find my way, so I stayed close to the wall of the cave to feel my way through the darkness. I continued to walk to the right along the wall until I saw the sunlight coming in the entrance of the cave. Feeling weak from the weight on my back, I sat down for a time to catch my breath and allow my eyes to adjust to the brightness of daylight.

The valley below and the fields beyond were pale in comparison to what I had seen in The Realm of the Fifth Dimension. I looked around hoping to see the old man waiting for me, but I couldn't see him anywhere. I decided to carry the door back to my house in the village and look for the old man. Tying the door securely with a rope I had in my leather pouch, I adjusted the weight on my back for balance, and walked toward the village. It was a goodly distance, so I stopped frequently to rest.

As I approached my village, the afternoon sun had faded into twilight. I stopped and stared. It looked familiar, and yet not. The people and their dress were different, and some of the houses looked different, too. There were more of them, and there were buildings I hadn't seen before. I was unable to recognize any of the people.

I hurried to my house on the edge of the village. A young girl holding a clay jug had just drawn water from the well and was carrying it on her shoulder toward the house. As she entered the gate, I approached her and asked her name. She told me her name was Reena, the daughter of Emil. Emil was my youngest brother. He was only a child when I left to go to the mountain. How could this be? I asked her to call her father, as I wished to speak with him.

Quickly, Emil came to the gate. His eyes widened and his mouth dropped open.

"Why, Kabir? Can it be you? Can this be my older brother?"

I could not believe what I saw! Yes, it was Emil, my youngest brother, now a young man. His round face and wide-set dark eyes were staring at me as he tried to reach out to embrace me. I lowered the door from my back and stood it against the gate, then reached out to embrace him.

"Emil! Tell me, what has happened?"

Needless to say, the time had changed into the future. My parents were dead. The old man who owed me the money was dead. Most of my friends were old. Only I remained as I am now. Of course, everyone asked about the Door of Symbols. No one would listen to my story about The Realm of the Fifth Dimension, a realm of true being, and the spirit named Light. People began to think I had gone mad, and avoided me more and more. I hid the door under the floor in my house.

Not knowing what to do, I decided to go to the monastery in the mountains to seek Master Djwal, the most enlightened holy man. On foot, I journeyed for one month seeking the only person who I believed would listen to my story. When I arrived at the ancient monastery, I spoke my request, and a brown robed monk escorted me down a long narrow hall. The monk stopped, tapped on a door, and we were asked to enter. I introduced myself, and the monk departed.

I entered the small room where Master Djwal greeted me from his pallet on the floor. He was a very old man, thin as a rail, with a long white straggly beard. He was barely able to move as he struggled to stand and greet me properly from his pallet. I was offered to pour two cups of tea from a nearby table with a single chair. Sitting on his bed with his tea, nodding his head now and then, he listened to my story.

He told me I had done a very grave deed, and I must seek guidance from one far wiser than he. I was to go to Egypt to the holy mountain in the Sinai Desert. He instructed me to take the Door of Symbols and seek guidance from the most holy monk who lived in the Monastery of Saint Catherine.

Kabir gasped. Barely able to speak, he whispered, "Now, my dear Captain Ashcroft... I am afraid... I may never make it there... I am so grateful for your kindness... and hospitality.... If I should die... do with the door as you wish..."

Kabir closed his eyes as his head sank into the pillow. A long breath of air released from his nostrils... his mouth parted... Kabir was dead.

After Kabir's burial, I began to search the Hindu scriptures looking for clues about the Door of Symbols. I found nothing. After several months, I began my journey into the Sinai Desert to find the monastery. After many days of my weary, hot travels, I arrived at the gates of Saint Catherine's Monastery. I inquired of a young monk upon my entering to take me to whomever I might tell my incredible story of the Door of Symbols.

After much deliberation with his superiors, one of the monks escorted me into the chapel where the monks prayed each morning. There, behind the altar, he led me down a long narrow passageway. At the end of the dimly lit passage was a dark wooden door. The young monk knocked lightly and waited. The door creaked open, and there stood an ancient hunchback monk dressed in a dark woolen robe, belted with a dingy white cord. His long wispy gray hair fell over his shoulders and his white beard straggled nearly to his waist. His gnarled fingers motioned for me to enter, which I did, leaving my escort to return from where he came. The ancient one motioned me toward a chair to sit.

The room was quite small. On one side of the room was a simple wood-framed bed with a dingy white cotton mattress stuffed with straw, and partly covered with a worn gray woolen blanket. A carved wooden crucifix hung above the bed. On the other side of the room stood one chair and a table heaped with books. The shelf above the table held a flickering oil lamp, and many pages of writings. He told me that he had expected me and was anxious to hear my story.

I have no idea how he knew I would be there... or even how long I was there. I never grew sleepy, hungry, or thirsty. The old man sat on the edge of his bed and didn't speak a word while he listened to all that I told him. When I had finished telling him about Kabir and the door, he stood, hobbled to the door, and pulled a chain to summon the monk who had escorted me to his chamber.

He then said to me, "I know of the Door of Symbols. It is written in the Akashic records of the earth. The Ancients have recorded all that lies here and beyond..from this dimension into the next. The past, the present, and the future are all one and the same. We humans are the ones on the journey. We only pass through the dimensions we choose for our soul's growth."

He then hobbled to the shelf of papers and shuffled through them. There, he located a papyrus with what appeared to be symbols or mysterious writing on it. He unrolled the document and placed it into a brown leather pouch, tying it with a leather cord. Handing me the pouch, he opened the door for me to leave.

"This will help you to understand. The secret is in the crystal," he said. He bowed stiffly from his hunched position. "Go in peace."

The same young monk was waiting to escort me back the way we had come. I turned to thank the old man only to see the door close behind me. I stood for a moment in silence, then followed the monk back through the passageway from behind the altar and out of the monastery.

Noah turned the page over. There was no writing on the back. He looked into the box and found nothing. Was that it? Was that all there was to the story? Noah began to search frantically through the trunk. He reached in and pulled out a photograph album, letters, and papers. At the bottom, he spotted a brown leather pouch tied with a leather cord, and lifted it out of the trunk.

Daylight was streaming through the sheer curtains as the sun peeked over the garden wall. Noah could hear the chirping of birds outside his window. Had he *really* sat there half the night reading what seemed to be an incredible story written by his great-grandfather? He held the pouch in his hand and untied the cord. Laying the cord on top of his pillow, he opened the flap. Inside, rolled with torn edges, was a papyrus darkened from the years. He slowly and ever so carefully unrolled it so he wouldn't tear the delicate page. It was a map covered with symbols and writing that Noah did not recognize. He held it in his hands, staring at it in disbelief.

"Noah?" He heard a light tapping and a whisper at his door. "Are you awake?" It was Hannah.

Noah carefully slipped the papyrus back into the pouch and slid it under his pillow. "Come on in, Hannah. I'm awake."

The door opened, and Hannah slipped in quietly, closing the door behind her.

"Everyone is still asleep," she whispered. "I woke up early and couldn't go back to sleep, so I thought I'd see if you were awake. You had gone to bed so early, I hoped you might be awake now."

"Yeah, I was awake at three this morning," said Noah, leaning back on his pillow.

"Wow! What *is* all this stuff? What all did you find here in this old trunk?" She knelt down on the floor beside the trunk and began to look through the clutter. "Look at these old photographs… and this old diary!"

Noah picked up the yellowed pages of the journal and held them out in his hands. "You will never guess what is written on these pages. After you read them, then I have my own story to tell you. I think we're about to uncover a mystery that has been in our family a very long time."

Hannah reached for the pages and began to read...

The Cave of Light

*N*oah left Hannah alone in his room to read the journal while he went downstairs to fix a snack before Mother and Father woke up.

Still holding the yellowed pages that she had finished reading, Hannah dropped her hands into her lap, and stared at the wall deep in thought. The journal written by their great-grandfather John Ashcroft was remarkable…and a little disturbing to her. Since she had no experience with the Door of Symbols, the journal seemed to be a story from someone's imagination.

Returning to his bedroom, Noah saw Hannah transfixed in thought. "Well, what do you think?" he asked as he sat down in the chair next to his desk.

Hannah didn't move. She just sat there on the edge of the bed holding the papers, staring at the wall. Finally, she said, "I really don't know what to make of this, Noah. Is this truly about that old door Mom and Dad placed in our garden wall?"

"Yes, I am sure beyond a doubt, that's how Great-grandfather Ashcroft acquired the door. You see, Hannah, I had an experience with the door when I was young. After Mom told us to never ever go through the door in the garden wall, well… I went anyway. I never told anyone about it. I was so scared, but I was lucky to have returned to the present time and not have been caught in a time warp. I only wanted to forget about it and never mentioned it to anyone. Now that these papers have revealed the story of the door, it has changed things. I think we should investigate the meaning of all this."

"Whoa, slow down! You're going way too fast for me. First of all, what experience are you talking about? What happened?"

Noah moved his chair closer to Hannah. He leaned forward to look into her eyes.

"Listen, what I am going to tell you is true. So, help me out by promising to keep this between you and me until I say it is okay to talk about it. Even Mom and Dad are not to know until we figure out what all of this is about. Promise?"

Hannah was always ready for an adventure, even if it was one that was only being told to her. She placed the faded yellow papers into the old chest, and leaned back on the pillows against the headboard of the bed.

"I promise," she answered, crossing her heart with her right index finger.

Noah took a deep breath and began. "Remember the summer I had received the natural science books for my birthday, and I was so interested in the concept of the metamorphosis of a butterfly? I had sculpted a butterfly out of clay. You came into my room wanting me to play a game, but I didn't want to play, so you, being you, slammed your fist down on my clay butterfly."

"Vaguely... I remember something like that," murmured Hannah, squinting her eyes as she tried to remember. "Oh, yes! I was feeling very sorry for what I had done, and I made up a game about butterflies. Then, I looked for you for the longest time in the garden to come play with me. You finally appeared, walking across the lawn from the far end of the garden."

"Yep, that's the time! That was the day I went through the door in the garden wall!"

"Well, what happened? Tell me about it!" Hannah leaned in toward her brother, waiting for him to answer.

Noah sat for a moment trying to think how to begin. A long time had passed since his experience.

"When you left my room that day, I was so upset that I took the clay off my table and was ready to take it to you to make you eat it!" Noah laughed. "Since I heard you lock your door instead, I decided I'd go downstairs and tell Mom about it. She was busy, so I ran off to the far end of the garden and crawled under that large lilac bush to be alone."

He walked to the window and held the sheer curtains aside, pointing to the bush. "See the one at the far end over there?" said Noah. "It's about as big as a tree now."

Hannah leaned forward so she could take a good look out the window. "Oh, yes, that one. Is *that* where the old door was placed, behind the lilac bush and climbing vines?"

"Yes, it's still there. I think Mom and Dad have even forgotten about it."

"Go on, Noah. Tell me what happened."

Noah returned to his chair and told the entire story of seeing the beautiful butterfly fly over the wall, opening the door to the other side, and chasing after it. He described the gray mist and the blue tunnel with the rose-colored light that led to the beautiful meadow of flowers and the lake surrounded by large oak trees with branches reaching up to the sky. He told her how the butterfly had turned into a being named Light, and how the being taught him about the crystal cages in which each person lives.

Light's words came back to him as he explained that a person does not know that another is a prisoner of his own thoughts in how he perceives the world around him. Even birds and animals lived in their own crystal cages of awareness. Noah described how Light allowed him to experience a dog's consciousness, and how he had also entered Hannah's crystal cage in order to understand her thoughts and feelings.

"That was *really* weird for me," Noah said with a laugh.

Hannah folded her arms over her chest and gave him a disgusted look. Noah continued, telling her how frightened he was that he might be caught in a time warp and not be able to return home. He still remembered the instructions Light had given him on how to take the crystal out of the center of the door so that he could return to normal time.

"I was never so frightened in my life, when that crystal kept slipping from my fingers, and I couldn't pry it from the door with the pointed end of a stick. Right when I was saying, 'Crystal sixty,' out it fell to the ground. I was afraid to turn around. When I did, I heard you yelling my name and saw you walking up the kitchen steps. Boy, I was never so glad to hear your voice! I would have forgiven you anything!" Noah chuckled and leaned back in his chair, waiting for Hannah's reaction. Hannah sat staring at Noah.

"Well, Hannah, don't you have anything to say? I've never seen you so speechless in my life," Noah said grinning from ear to ear.

Hannah stiffened her body, and with a stern look stared Noah right in the eyes.

"Noah, how do I know that you aren't lying and telling me all of this to trick me? I wouldn't put it past you one bit to get me to buy into this story just so you could have a good laugh after I go along with it. Not on your life! You just read those papers from Great-grandfather Ashcroft and made up all of this just to see what reaction I'd have. Then you'd play me along like a fish on a hook. No way! I am not falling for this one minute!" Hannah jumped up from the bed and reached for the doorknob.

Startled by her reaction, Noah jumped up from his chair to block her from leaving the room. "Wait! Wait a minute, hear me out! I'm not finished!"

Hannah tried to push on past him, then stopped. "I think I've heard enough!" she yelled.

"No, wait! There's more! Please, Hannah, sit down. I can prove to you or at least try to convince you that I'm telling the truth. I know my story sounds like a fantasy. That's why I never told anyone, not even Mom or Dad. I was sure no one would believe me. Now that we have these papers, there is something else I want to show you."

Hannah hesitated for a moment before releasing a frustrated sigh. "All right, fine, but it better be good! I'm getting hungry and I want to go downstairs and eat breakfast."

"Okay, okay, but please sit down for just a few more minutes," Noah urged, gesturing toward the bed.

Hannah sat, and Noah reached under his pillow and pulled out the worn leather pouch. "Look at this. This was also in the chest. This pouch was given to Great-grandfather by the old monk in the monastery on Mount Sinai."

"What's in it?" she asked, as she reached for the pouch.

"Be careful with the papyrus. It's very old and tends to crumble."

Hannah delicately removed the papyrus, and began to unroll it carefully.

"Wow, look at these symbols! Some of them are quite faded. And this writing... I've never seen anything like this. What do you think it is, Noah?" She ran her finger across the page.

Noah grabbed his magnifying glass off the desk. "Here, let me take a look with this glass so I can see more detail. Once I saw writing similar to this in a National Geographic Magazine. I'd say it looks like it could be Sanskrit. It's supposed to be the oldest known written language from India. I wish that we knew someone who could read this for us." Noah moved the magnifying glass back and forth across the parchment. "And look at these symbols! Really strange... Some look like trees, and here's a kind of spiral or snake. Look here, this one seems to be a heart, and this one looks like a cross. I must try to find someone who might know about these symbols and this kind of writing."

"Noah, you'll be returning to Cambridge soon. England has a large East Indian population. Maybe you could find someone who can read Sanskrit writing and have them interpret what's written here. Should we tell Mom and Dad what we've found?" asked Hannah.

"Let's wait awhile. We'll put the written journal of Great-grandfather's back in the box, and leave it in the chest. I want to take this papyrus to England and try to find someone who can interpret the writing and symbols. I'll carry it on me to make sure it stays safe."

Hannah was slipping Great-grandfather's journal back into its box and placing it into the trunk when she remembered something she had read.

"Wait a minute. Remember what Great-grandfather Ashcroft wrote about what the old monk had said to him as he was leaving the monk's quarters?"

"What? What are you referring to?"

She stood, pacing the floor trying to remember. "The old monk's last words were, 'remember, the secret is in the crystal,'" Hannah quoted. "The secret is in the crystal. What does that mean?"

Noah walked over to the bookcase and reached up on the top shelf for the box that held the crystal.

"Hannah, this is the grand finale to the story that I told you. This is my proof: *the* crystal. I took it out of the door. This must be what the old monk was talking about."

Noah and Hannah sat on the edge of his bed. Hannah leaned toward the box as Noah lifted the lid. There it was, like a diamond looking back at them. They both stared at it a moment before Noah took it out. When rotated in Noah's fingers, the crystal caught the light of the morning sun. The fissures inside the crystal emitted rays of gold and pink and blue.

"Oh, let me hold it," said Hannah in amazement as she took the crystal in her hands and began to turn it about. "The light seems to come from within. Look how the different colors sparkle as the light reflects from it." They took turns looking at the crystal until they heard their names being called.

"Noah! Hannah! Breakfast is ready!" Dad called from the bottom of the stairs. "You two better get down here if you want something to eat!"

"We'll be right there!" shouted Hannah from the door of the bedroom. Noah slipped the crystal back into the box, and was ready to place it up on the shelf when Hannah stopped him.

"You'll be leaving in a couple of days. May I keep it in my room until I go back to the dance studio? I'll put it back on top of your bookcase when I leave."

"Sure. I know this has been quite a morning for you," Noah said, waving the leather pouch in the air. "I hope now you'll believe my story. I want to get to the bottom of this. You'll have lots to think about, and maybe later we can work on this together. Come on, let's go see what Mom has fixed for breakfast."

The time came for Noah to return to Cambridge and continue his studies. Hannah, Mom, and Dad drove Noah to the airport. They entered, waited for Noah to check in, and said their good-byes at Passport Control. As Noah passed through the control check, Hannah called out, "Bye, Noah! Have a good year! Don't forget to look for someone who reads Sanskrit!"

"What was that Sanskrit comment all about?" Dad asked as they walked from the air terminal to the parking lot.

"Oh, that? That was just a private joke between us. Something about not understanding my writing." Hannah shrugged and turned toward her mom to change the subject.

That night, when Hannah was lying in her bed thinking about the previous conversation with Noah and the symbols written on the parchment, she reached for the box on her nightstand. Carefully, she took out the crystal and studied the facets on each side, trying to determine how this crystal could hold the mystery that the old monk spoke about. She held it in her right hand as she pondered the possibilities. Her hand seemed to pulsate while holding the crystal. Then without even thinking about it, she raised the crystal to her eye to see the colors radiating within. Closing her left eye, she held the crystal to her right and stared deep within it.

Hannah was able to see the matrix as it appeared to move and float like a white fog rolling in from the sea. She held the crystal steady with her elbow propped on her chest as she watched the white mist appear and disappear in the crystal. A tunnel of bluish light appeared and formed around a center of pinkish light. Looking deeper and deeper within, a vortex of light appeared and became brighter and brighter. Hannah felt as though she was being drawn in and pulled through a tunnel into a blinding white light. She closed her eyes...

When she opened them, she found herself sitting on the floor of a crystal cave. The atmosphere was pleasant and the floor cool to the touch. Each crystal formation sparkled and reflected the colors of the rainbow. There seemed to be a peaceful, harmonious frequency around her, one that gave her a complete sense of well-being. Sensing no fear whatsoever, she felt as though she was in a beautiful dream. Hannah stood up and walked among the crystals, delighting in the shapes and radiating colors of each one. She noticed that when she moved from side to side, the colors in the crystals changed in response to her movements, almost as if they were trying to communicate with her.

As she walked farther into the cave, it was not long before she came across a huge crystal in the shape of a door. The light from the door seemed to draw her into and through it. There, she found herself in a beautiful domed room with small crystals of every shape and size extending from the ceiling. The light catching each one created a rainbow of dancing colors all around the room. Twirling around, looking at the colors flowing over the room, Hannah caught sight of a beautiful being sitting on a crystal throne, smiling at Hannah's delight.

"Oh!" Hannah suddenly came to a stop, trying to catch her balance from twirling. "Hello. Who are you?"

Smiling, the being stood and descended the throne toward Hannah.

"My name is Light. This is where I live, in the Cave of Light," she said, gesturing about the room. "Welcome, Hannah, to my realm. This is the realm where you began your journey to Earth, and where you will return from your journey."

"How... How do you know my name?" Hannah asked, feeling confused. "You speak as though you expected me."

"Dearest Hannah, I know all souls by their Earth names. Before you descended into the Third Dimension, I am the one who kissed you good-bye and sealed your lips of the Knowledge of Heaven. Earth is where you need to go to experience the feelings and emotions of that dimension. Your journey in life is to find your way back to your heavenly home. Each soul here makes a contract to learn life's lessons and to contribute something to the evolution. You see, the original blueprint, or Divine Plan is held here. In order for the earth to return to its perfect state, each soul must discover his or her mission. The mission is to help raise the collective consciousness of mankind on Earth. Then we all will rise into this heavenly dimension of love, peace, and harmony: the perfected creation of the Creator."

Hannah stood in awe at Light's ethereal beauty. Her countenance projected a shimmering light and her gown sparkled in tones of pale pink, gold, lavenders, and blues. Her pale hair flowed and sparkled around her shoulders. Lavender almond-shaped eyes and her sweet smile released a radiating essence of love.

"Wow, Light, that is truly an awesome idea, but how does it work? I can't imagine how human beings could complete such an amazing task. They are so busy living in fear and want, I don't see how that could ever come about."

"Perhaps not in one human lifetime, but all positive, loving thoughts and actions are cumulative. Come with me and I will show you," she said. Light led the way to a large crystal window.

"Sit here. Look straight at this window and tell me what you see."

Hannah sat down on a bench of white crystal. It felt warm and comfortable. She was surprised at herself, how calm and accepting she was with what she was experiencing when she had dismissed her brother's story so quickly. It just seemed natural to her to be sitting there... taking it all in.

Staring at the window, she saw a pink glow appear. This was followed by a pale yellow, and then a pale lavender and blue emerged as though she were watching the coming of dawn. When the light became brighter, the colors disappeared. As though she were in space, Hannah was able to see Planet Earth in the distance. There it was: a beautiful blue planet with an aura of pale light surrounding it like a jewel suspended in the black void of space.

"Oh, how beautiful Earth looks from here! I've seen photos of the moon and it looks dead and lifeless, but the earth... it's so radiant! I never thought of our planet actually being alive, a truly living planet. It supports all life as we know it. That's our home! It's where I live!" exclaimed Hannah.

"As you know, dear Hannah, all humans were created to be stewards of the earth. Your religions teach this. Humans are the bridge between the life on Earth, and life of higher realms. Your purpose is to serve the Creator and His creation. I will show you a fast sequence of pictures over millions of years to demonstrate how the plan was forgotten."

Hannah watched the window intently. The picture changed, and there was the Earth in all of her glory, a perfect garden called Eden. The first humans sat under the Tree of Life in peace and harmony. Each day, they walked and talked with the Creator. All beauty and abundance was theirs to partake in. They received sustenance freely from the Tree of Life and communicated with the animals and all of nature.

But the image changed as darkness, envy, and deceit crept into the minds of humans, followed by fear and greed, causing the now neglected Garden to show signs of lifelessness and decay. The colors faded.

Man plowed the earth, killed the animals, and cut down the forests. He polluted the streams, rivers, and oceans. Overtime, the sky became smudged with a permanent grayness of smoke and pollution. Parts of the earth were soon covered with cement and holes were dug deep into the earth's crust to draw out her precious life's liquid. The minerals that kept her energies balanced in order to give sustenance to growing life were removed. Her soil was poisoned. Seeds of plants and trees were altered, reducing its life force to sustain living creatures. Rivers were diverted and dammed to create lakes, reducing still more energy. Through the corruption of mankind, the descending cycles perverted the harmony as they decided to use the earth for their own selfish purposes. Wars were declared across the land. People became more and more fearful and angry because they didn't feel the peace and harmony that they had known in their hearts. Even the words "love" and "Creator" were sneered at. "Wealth" and "power" became persuasive words.

These negative energies spread throughout the world causing tremendous destruction. Earth began to tremble and shake, causing earthquakes to try to ease the pain and remove the hurt. Volcanoes and forest fires burned as she released the suffering from within her core. Again, rains poured and floods came, trying to cleanse our dear Mother Earth. Finally, man placed huge hydrogen bombs into the bowels of the planet, and exploded them to the horror of all creation in the galaxy.

Hannah sat with tears in her eyes, shocked at what she saw. Then she saw angels appearing and surrounding the earth; millions of them saddened by the fate of this jewel in the Milky Way Galaxy. A great clarion call went forth from the Creator to all souls in every corner of the cosmos to volunteer their help. Souls from every part of the universe heard the Creator's call. Many volunteered and came to help heal the sufferings of the blue planet.

Dearest new souls were born, each one holding the Divine Plan within their hearts. They carried a special blueprint within their soul to give service to Planet Earth. These souls were lovingly held in their parents' arms, and grew daily to remember the purpose of their being.

To Hannah's horror, standing next to the parents were dark mysterious forms waiting to devour and destroy the souls of these little light beings with drugs, alcohol, greed, and power. This was intended to distort their thinking and divert their divine purpose in life. These dark forces held the illusion of deceitful promises over these young soul's minds in order to entice them away from remembering their mission on Earth.

The picture changed once more. Many souls being pulled away by the darkness became awakened by a bright light, a light shining somewhere inside their hearts. These souls began to remember and recreate "the Plan." Even without knowing it, the light within began to shine brighter until love flowed from their hearts. This love connected with other hearts. Soon, a bridge of light began to form, and beautiful colors of light permeated the darkness. As more light and love flowed from the Creator into the hearts of mankind, darkness slowly dissipated from the earth.

Seeds of light had been planted by the children of man. They grew, and life renewed abundantly on Earth. A rainbow bridge formed from man's heart to the Creator's heart. Angels appeared again and blessings flowed from the Divine Source to mankind. Once again, life and beauty were restored on Earth.

After eons of time, all of Creation in the universe leapt for joy as Earth was restored to her golden age of peace, harmony, and unity. Mother Earth ascended into the heavenly dimension. People of the earth were blessed beyond their greatest dreams. They truly walked and talked with the Creator, and the Tree of Life grew once again in the Garden. Hannah saw the earth suspended in the void as a radiant blue planet of light.

Finally, the light within the window began to dim into the pale pink, blues, and lavender of twilight, then disappeared. The window returned to crystal. Hannah sat for a moment, completely absorbed in her thoughts of what she had witnessed. With tears welling up in her eyes, she turned to Light.

"Light? Are we truly *the children of light* who are to return to Earth during this time?"

"Oh, yes, you are! This is a critical time on Earth, a time for awakening to the Spirit within. This is a time to become aware of your destiny by understanding your power to create. You *can* make a difference. Remember, you are children of the Creator. This love is the strongest force on the planet. There is nothing stronger. It is the cohesive element that sustains all life. Even when there appears to be disharmony, it can be the emotion for changing the tone of disharmony into harmony."

"I'll never forget what you've shown me, Light," Hannah said, feeling more determined than ever before. "Now, I understand that I must truly look within to find answers to my questions, and to seek my purpose in life. I am able to see my fellow man in a different way, and I won't judge, criticize, or mock what I don't understand. Truly, in this life, we are each on a journey together. We must support one another so we'll be able to restore the Divine Plan."

"Yes, dear Hannah, I know you will. You will return here again one day, walking into the light with a big smile on your face. Remember. Remember. *Remember who you are*!" Light smiled, holding her delicate hands out toward Hannah.

Hannah took a deep breath and rolled over on her side. The crystal hit the floor, the thud echoed in the silent room. Startled, Hannah awoke and sat up in bed.

"What was that?" She looked around the room. The light was still on. She looked at her clock. Had she slept most of the night? I *don't remember going to sleep. I was with Light in the crystal cave. I was shown the past and future of the world. Why, I can remember every detail that I saw and heard,* she pondered.

Hannah leaned down and picked up the crystal. She held it in her hand, thinking about what she had experienced. Did she really fall asleep and dream that dream, or was there some magic power in the crystal? Did it hold the wisdom and knowledge of the universe? Was Light a figment of her imagination, or the spirit living within the crystal? One thing Hannah knew was that this was not an ordinary crystal; perhaps it wasn't even an Earth crystal. It must have come from somewhere… Hannah placed the crystal back into the box and closed the lid.

"I must find out what this crystal is, and where it came from," she said to herself.

Left of the Sun and
North of the Moon

*H*annah returned to the dance studio in New York. Weeks passed, and the longer days of summer were welcomed. She so longed to take time off and enjoy a summer vacation.

Late one afternoon after leaving the studio, she walked to the subway, took train number 9 to her accustomed stop, and hurriedly walked the remaining distance to her small apartment. Ascending the front steps, she stopped outside the door to open her mailbox. She noticed a letter with a foreign stamp on it and checked the return address. Sure enough, it was from her brother. She was eager to read it. Hannah unlocked the door to her apartment, tossed her dance bag onto the sofa, and sat down to open the letter.

Dear Hannah,

Have I got news for you! Arjun, one of the Indian students in my geology class, recently invited me to an Indian restaurant. I spoke to him about finding someone who could read ancient Sanskrit, and he mentioned it immediately to his friend, the waiter, who works there. As luck would have it, the waiter was certain his grandfather, Mr. Singh, would be able to decipher the writing.

Later, I spoke by phone with Mr. Singh, and when I told him of the papyrus that I found in Great-grandfather's trunk, he became very interested.

Hannah, could you take a week or two off from the dance studio and fly to London to meet me? We'll go visit Mr. Singh together. Bring the crystal with you. Telephone me at 00-44-1-755-89231 with the date and time of your arrival. I can't wait to see you!

Love,
Noah

Hannah laid the letter down on the sofa and went into the kitchen to make a cup of peppermint tea. While pouring the boiling water over the leaves, she mentally planned how she would first go to her parents' home, and then to England. She knew Mom and Dad would probably fuss at her for not spending more time with them, saying, "Why couldn't Noah come to our house where we could all be together?"

Sipping her tea, Hannah replaced the cup on the saucer and removed the calendar from her desk. She selected the dates, and then telephoned Mom and Dad. She had to make sure Mom had not discarded the box holding the crystal. She wanted to carry the crystal with her to be sure it was safe.

Checking the dates off on the calendar, Hannah called the dance studio to see if they could let her take a couple of weeks off from classes as there was an important family matter to take care of. Thankfully, it was possible. She telephoned Mom and Dad to let them know she planned to visit for a few days, and then called the airline to make reservations. Those days were open, and the tickets were reserved. *Great!* she thought.

That evening Hannah picked up the telephone to call her brother.

"Hello?"

"Hi, Noah! This is Hannah!"

"Hey, Hannah! Did you receive my letter?"

"Of course I did silly, and I'm on my way. I've booked the airline reservations, but first I'll stop to see Mom and Dad. I'll be sure to pick up the crystal and leave for England from there."

"Great! What day will you be arriving, and which airport?"

Hannah's enthusiasm was apparent in her voice. "I arrive on British Airways at 4:00 p.m., Saturday after next. I fly into Heathrow Airport. I am so anxious to see you, Noah! This sounds very exciting, and I can't wait to meet Mr. Singh."

"I can't wait for you to come here! I've already talked by telephone to Mr. Singh, and he seems to be a very interesting old gentleman and very knowledgeable. I'll be waiting at the gate for you the Saturday after next. Have a good flight!"

Hannah busied herself with preparations for the trip. The visit with her parents was pleasant. As always, Hannah loved to be home with Mom and Dad. She loved her mom's home cooking, and enjoyed lounging around in her childhood bedroom, looking at photos in her scrapbook and reminiscing. The crystal was still where she had placed it back on the bookshelf in Noah's bedroom. Hannah reached for the crystal and placed it in her backpack to ensure she would not forget it when she left.

The time came to leave for England. Hannah had said her "good-byes" at the airport with hugs and kisses to her parents. Now she was settled on the plane and relaxed in her seat. Right on time the plane lifted off the runway. Midway during the flight, Hannah reached into her backpack and felt around for the crystal: still there.

Cradling it in the palm of her hand, she could feel a pulsing effect that flowed up her forearm to her elbow. Hopefully, the mystery of the crystal would be resolved by the time she returned home. Feeling drowsy, she reclined her seat, closed her eyes, and fell asleep.

When the plane landed, Hannah disembarked and walked to the waiting area. Noah was there to meet her. They greeted and hugged, and were so excited to see one another. Noah could not wait to get right to the heart of the matter, telling Hannah all about his new friend at the restaurant and his grandfather, Mr. Singh.

"Wait a minute, Noah! Hold on, you're walking too fast! I need to get my luggage, and we need to go somewhere where we can talk so I can take this all in," Hannah said, trying to keep up with Noah's fast pace.

"You're right. I guess waiting all this time has made me impatient. I need to calm down. We'll pick up your luggage, and take the subway to my friend's flat in London. I hope you won't mind sharing a flat with two guys. I'll sleep on the sofa, and he said you could have the cot in the small bedroom. Arjun works evenings at his father's restaurant and attends classes during the day. That means he usually returns late in the evening, so most of the time, while you are here, we'll have his flat to ourselves."

"That sounds fine to me. There's my suitcase!" Hannah shouted, spotting her luggage on the carousel.

"Wow, this is a heavy suitcase!" Noah teased as he pulled it off the belt and headed for the underground Tube. "What do you have in here, the kitchen sink?" Hannah gave him one of her famous, "*Not funny, Noah*," looks as they headed for the underground Tube.

A few minutes and escalators later, the two found themselves in the brightly lit underground Tube. They did not have to wait long as the red and white train sped silently towards the platform.

"Here comes our train now. It'll take us to Ladbroke Grove. That's the area where Arjun lives. We may have to walk a bit. Thank goodness your suitcase has wheels on it," Noah smiled.

Hannah returned one of her "fake" smiles. "How long will it take?"

"Probably about forty minutes. You be sure to get some rest when we get there. I can't wait to go see Mr. Singh. You *do* have the crystal, don't you?" Noah asked in a serious voice.

This was Hannah's chance to do the teasing. Squinting her eyes, she scratched her head before shrugging her shoulders,

"Oh... I thought I was forgetting something," murmured Hannah.

"That is not funny... You'd better be teasing." When she wouldn't answer him right away, he looked her straight in the eyes. "Tell me you have it!"

Hannah knew when Noah gave her that look that she better not tease. Besides, she was too tired to get into it with her brother. "Yes, I do have it. Don't get upset."

When the train stopped at Ladbroke Grove, they got off. After walking a couple blocks, they entered a door located around the side of a brick building. Noah pulled some keys out of his coat pocket and unlocked the door.

"This is Arjun's flat," Noah said as they entered the apartment. "His family hasn't been in England very long. His father and uncle are part owners of an Indian restaurant on Portobello Road. Arjun will take us to meet his grandfather tomorrow and that is when our adventure will begin. For now, let's get settled in and then grab a bite to eat."

In the morning, Hannah awoke early. She could hear occasional snores and snorts coming from the other rooms. She decided to unpack a few things and get dressed, hoping that her stirring around might wake the two sleepyheads. Within the hour, the boys were awake and dressed, and Hannah was introduced to Arjun.

"My grandfather is expecting us around 11:00 this morning. I will take you there. However, I will have to leave you so I can get to my classes," Arjun explained as he finished the last of his hot tea, then placed his cup and saucer on the coffee table.

"That's not a problem," Noah answered. "I know my way around London quite well, so we will have no problem finding our way about. Thank you for helping us out."

"We are so looking forward to meeting with Mr. Singh," Hannah commented. "Noah has told me what an interesting gentleman he is. And thank you for sharing your flat with us, Arjun. It is most kind of you." Hannah smiled as she gathered up the cups to return to the kitchen.

Portobello Road was chock-full of people with vendors and shops lining the streets. Crowds were beginning to gather as the three friends walked along looking in the various store-fronts and listening to street vendors hawking their goods. Soon, Arjun stopped, opened a black wrought-iron gate, and entered. In front of them stood an old, white Victorian house with a large front porch.

Walking up the steps, they could see a bay window, filed with antiques, dominating the front of the house. Gold-colored tassels which held back burgundy brocade drapes framed a fascinating display of Indian antiques that could be seen in the window. As they entered, Hannah's eyes jumped from bronze statues of Buddha and Shiva to old furniture. An old chest filled with colorful, richly embroidered pillows, were all attractively arranged.

"This is my Aunt Anjali's house and antique store. She is probably in the back with a customer. I will take you right away downstairs where Grandfather is expecting us, and then I will be on my way. I don't want to be late for class." Arjun smiled as he led them down the steps.

When they entered the downstairs living quarters, Mr. Singh slowly stood from his chair.

"Namaste," greeted Arjun folding his hands to his chest.

"Namaste, Arjun." They bowed and then hugged each other.

"You remember Noah who telephoned you. And this is his lovely sister, Hannah."

"Namaste." Mr. Singh warmly greeted Hannah and Noah with a bow before he shook their hands. After they were introduced and had exchanged pleasantries, Arjun went on his way. Mr. Singh offered Noah and Hannah a comfortable place on the sofa, then left to fetch hot tea and biscuits.

After a short visit and refreshments, Mr. Singh leaned back in his overstuffed chair. "Noah, I understand you are looking for someone who can read Sanskrit writing," Mr. Singh said as he reached for his reading glasses on a small end table beside him.

"Yes, that's correct. I found a very old inscription in a chest that once belonged to my great-grandfather. I am not sure, but I think it may be ancient Sanskrit or some form of Hindu writing. My great-grandfather was a sea captain for the Royal British Navy, and possibly had many adventures in the Near East and India. Perhaps you can help me."

"Hmm, perhaps I can. I am a historian of ancient cultures and religions. My eyes aren't as sharp as they used to be, and my memory seems to be fading; however, I will see what I can do," the old man assured, moving aside his cup and saucer.

Noah reached into his book bag and drew out the leather pouch holding the yellowed papyrus. Hannah cleared away the cups and saucers to make room so Noah could spread out the papyrus on the table for Mr. Singh to see.

"Let's take a look and see what we have here," the old man remarked.

Mr. Singh was a rather small man with a frail looking body. His head full of white hair and deep, penetrating dark eyes gave an impression of intense seriousness. He also wore brown leather Indian slippers with turned up toes, and his starched white Nehru jacket reminded Hannah of white pajamas.

Hannah looked around the room noticing the dark, heavy-looking, carved furniture and bright red-orange silk pillows on the sofa and chairs. A small fireplace at the far end of the room warmed the morning air. The smell of sandalwood incense lingered, aided by a gentle breeze in the stairway, causing hanging brass bells to stir, evoking soft tinkling sounds.

Mr. Singh bent over the table. His hands were a bit shaky as he extended them toward the table, delicately smoothing out the lines in the papyrus. He bowed his head to look more closely at the writing. He adjusted the glasses on his face, and then froze.

Noah and Hannah didn't move. They looked only at Mr. Singh, to the writing on the papyrus, and then back at Mr. Singh, as they waited for a response.

Moments passed. Mr. Singh cleared his throat. His eyes were intense as he looked up from the writing, first at Noah, then Hannah. His mouth quivered as he tried to form the words, which wouldn't come out.

Finally, he stammered, "Wh… Where did you say this came from?" His hands shook as he reached for a magnifying glass lying next to the lamp on the side table.

Noah, sensing the tension in the air, swallowed hard and repeated,

"As I mentioned, this papyrus belonged to my great-grand-father, Captain Ashcroft. He was a captain in the Royal Navy during the late 1800's. I have a journal of his, and he tells of receiving this papyrus from an old monk living in the monastery on Mount Sinai. I recently found it in the trunk that my great-grandmother kept. When she died, the trunk was passed on to my grandmother. Recently my grandmother, Lucia, died, and now the trunk is in our parents' house."

Mr. Singh was busy going over each section of the writing, muttering and gasping as though he had not heard a single word Noah had said. Noah and Hannah remained quiet until Mr. Singh finally paused and looked up at them. He laid the magnifying glass down, and leaned back in his chair. He looked at the writings, then at Noah, and then fixed his eyes on Hannah.

In a cold demanding voice, Mr. Singh asked, "Do either one of you have the crystal?"

Startled, Noah and Hannah looked at each other. They hadn't counted on that question being asked right away. Neither spoke for a moment.

"We know where it is," Noah finally said. "Why? What can you tell us about it?"

Mr. Singh relaxed in his chair. "This is the most remarkable piece of antiquity I have ever come across," he said, pointing toward the table, and bowing his head as if in reverence.

"This is something one only reads about in legends. It's like finding a piece of Noah's Ark or the Ark of the Covenant." Again, the old man bowed his head, closed his eyes, and sighed.

Noah could not stand the suspense one minute longer. "Tell us! What is it?!" He blurted out. "Don't leave us in suspense!"

Hannah was spellbound. She felt this was totally beyond her comprehension, and it was getting too deep for her, so she decided just to sit back, listen, and not to say a word.

Mr. Singh stood up and walked over to the bookcase. He ran his fingers along a row of leather-bound books until he located the right one. Pulling it off of the shelf, he blew dust off the top and wiped the cover with his sleeve.

"I am going to need some help with this one," he said, looking at the book he held in his hand. Bringing it over to the table, he sat down, and opened it, thumbing through the pages.

Noah could see the title, *The Emerald Tablets*. An engraving in gold of the Egyptian God Thoth, symbolized by the Ibis and Ankh, was on the brown leather cover.

"Ah... Here it is," the old man said, and he began to read. *"All symbols are but keys to doors leading to the truth. Many times the door is not opened because the key seems too great. If we can understand that all keys, all material manifestations, are but extensions of the Great Law, we will begin to develop the vision which will enable us to penetrate Beyond the Door."*

The old man lay the book beside him on the sofa, and again, leaned over the table. He looked first at Hannah and then Noah.

"What you have here is a very ancient inscription or codex on papyrus, one that has been inscribed from the ancient writings of possibly the Atlantean language," he began. "These writings were kept in the Halls of Amenti under the Great Pyramid of Giza. This was part of an initiation rite in the Spiritual Mystery Schools, and was for the spiritual advancement of an adept wishing to become enlightened. Only those who had the "light" within were able to advance. The characters you see here respond to the attuned thoughts released from the associated mental vibrations in the brain of the reader. This releasing opens the treasury of knowledge and wisdom within."

Noah and Hannah looked at each other, and then at the old man. Becoming more perplexed, Noah questioned, "What does that mean, and how do you know that?"

Mr. Singh sighed as he again sat back in his chair. "As I mentioned before, I am a historian of ancient cultures and religions. I have studied the Naacal writings from the earliest civilization during the Lemurian epoch, which is believed to be very similar to Sanskrit. I have also studied ancient Hebrew, Aramaic, Greek, and Egyptian hieroglyphics, which are considered similar to the Atlantean symbols. I can only tell you what I know. The rest is left to those far wiser than I."

Still trying to make sense of what he had heard, Noah asked, "Tell us, where did this papyrus come from? What do these symbols mean? And what does the crystal have to do with any of it?"

"Let me start from the beginning of what I am trying to tell you. You may be here longer than you planned. Would you care for another cup of tea?"

Both Noah and Hannah felt they would jump up out of their seats if they had to wait a minute longer to find out what was written on the papyrus.

Trying not to appear impatient, Hannah replied, "Thank you, but no. I have had quite enough tea, thank you. Please go on."

Mr. Singh adjusted the pillow at the small of his back and began.

"The writings tell of a time fifteen and a half million years ago when a meteor came from the far reaches of the galaxy, passing by the left side of the sun, and the north side of the moon, hitting the earth. This meteor was unusual because it was not composed of the usual meteorite substance, but of a lighter density. When it hit the earth at a very great speed, the meteor fused with the crust of the earth creating beautiful, sparkling crystals of purest quality. This united the wisdom of the cosmos to the matrix of the earth. Soon, it was discovered that the energy from these crystals imparted a higher knowledge to certain individuals who wore it over their hearts."

Mr. Singh paused as he noticed Noah's eyes widening in amazement. Adjusting his glasses on the bridge of his nose, the old man continued.

"These crystals became highly sought after. All those who wished to reach the highest knowledge searched for a piece of crystal from this meteor. However, only those who were born from the gift of true love were able to receive wisdom from this unusual stone. This meteor, a great gift from the universe, was sent for the true seekers of light. In Atlantis, this crystal was used as the capstone on the Great Pyramids of initiation into the highest Mysteries Schools of Wisdom and the Laws of the Universe. It was also placed into the temple doors of their most sacred buildings."

Again, Mr. Singh paused, looking directly at Noah, and then Hannah, trying to mentally register their comprehension from the astonished look on their faces. Leaning forward in his chair, he went on.

"Legend tells us that this meteor that came from the left of the sun and north of the moon created great envy and greed among those who were not able to receive its natural powers. Those who were not pure of heart could suffer great tragedies if they tried to deface or steal any part of a door with a crystal.

"As time passed, the dark forces of mankind decided to use the great crystals for greed and power. They elicited the help of some of the high priests in Atlantis who were illegitimately ordained for this nefarious purpose. Huge crystals from the meteor were confiscated and placed on towers all over the land in order to use its energy for evil. At first, this energy was used to light homes, run transportation, and communication networks to ease the consciousness of those who were skeptical regarding the use of power.

"Then the evil minds used it to control and punish the inhabitants of the land. They would use the force for mind control, to destroy cities, and entire countries by creating earthquakes and tidal waves. The greed for more and more energy to accomplish these evil deeds built greater and greater intensity within the planet. This mighty force from the crystals was so intense that it began to loosen the crust of the Earth. This force created a catastrophic earthquake, sinking Atlantis bit by bit until, at last, it went asunder. "The great Atlantis, in a day and a night," as Plato tells us, "sunk beneath the sea."

The old man leaned back in his chair, closed his eyes, and sighed as though he, himself, was able to remember that catastrophic event. Pausing, he removed his glasses and rubbed his eyes before he continued.

"This papyrus we have before us must be studied by those minds possessing the highest knowledge as it very well could be from the great library of Alexandria, Egypt." Mr. Singh pointed to the papyrus. "This could be the greatest find in history! You must protect it at all costs and see to it that only historians of high integrity have access to it. If you like, I will try to contact someone from the Museum of Ancient Antiquities to give you advice," he offered.

Noah and Hannah were stunned to hear the magnitude of importance contained in the document.

"And what about the crystal?" Hannah asked, remembering Noah's and her experiences with it.

The old man looked at her with intensity, guessing she might be the one who knew its whereabouts.

"I cannot say for sure. I only know it would be the rarest gem on the face of the earth. Anyone who owned this crystal would hold the secrets of the cosmos; left of the sun and north of the moon. Perhaps coming as far away as the center of the Milky Way Galaxy. You told me that you two know the whereabouts of this crystal? I would love to have the privilege of holding such a treasure in my hand," he said, smiling first at Noah and then at Hannah. They both tensed when they noticed a faint glint of covetousness in Mr Singh's piercing black eyes.

"Yes, we did tell you that," Noah quickly answered before Hannah could open her mouth. "It's in a safety deposit box, and we would need to get permission to open it."

Hannah turned to look at him, and felt Noah's foot nudge hers under the coffee table.

Not saying a word, the old man caught the glimpse of deceit between the two. He carried on the conversation in a congenial manner.

"You asked about the crystal, and I will tell you what I am able to read that is written on the papyrus. The symbols indicate a door or doorway to somewhere. A place of '*all knowing,*' and the crystal part is a riddle." He began to read slowly.

"Gently hold me in your hand.
I am a window to another land.
From a different time to a world afar;
a journey to our distant Star.
When you hold me at the start,
you must find that same place within your heart."

As though in deep thought, the old man looked up over his glasses at the two young people sitting before him. He remembered something else, and again, his gnarled finger slowly followed the writing across the worn page.

"Within each is a higher eternal self. There is a window that offers a great gift connecting you to your soul. This is important in helping to gain an expanded awareness of life. To the extent you are able to communicate with this part of yourself, you can receive wisdom, comfort, and guidance. The heart is the portal to the mind. Awareness, realization, and commitment are the three keys that open this portal to higher consciousness."

Laying the magnifying glass down, he spoke haltingly as if in deep thought, trying to unravel the riddle connected to the crystal.

"When looking into the crystal, there must be a window of sorts, or shape within the crystal that reflects a frequency back into one's eye. This frequency could connect brain cells or codes opening the 'third eye,' the wisdom center, or some other part of man's consciousness that enables him to remember his connection to the Creator. There have been many masters from the beginning of time reminding us that we are only travelers upon this earth...teaching us how to live, bringing us back to the Creator. This crystal, this stone from the cosmos, could be a way shower for the twenty-first century."

Leaning forward, Mr. Singh asked enthusiastically, "Could you possibly bring to me this crystal, so I might have a look at it?"

Noah squirmed in his chair.

"I'll see what I can do, Mr. Singh," he answered as he leaned over to retrieve the papyrus from the table. "Is there anything more you can tell us about this? This has been such a rewarding morning for us. Hannah and I will have so much to discuss, and, of course, our parents will want to hear everything you have told us."

Mr. Singh smiled and thanked them both for the great privilege of having the opportunity to study such a rare manuscript of "outstanding significance," as he called it.

"If I am able to help you again in any way, please don't hesitate to contact me," he added.

Noah stood to shake Mr. Singh's hand.

"I'll take this with me, and we'll pursue the information you have given to us. We want to find out as much as we can. The knowledge and help you shared with us has certainly been an eye opener to what I've experienced."

Hannah had not yet told Noah of her experience with the crystal. She had nearly forgotten to mention it. When Mr. Singh began to speak of the window in the crystal, she could barely contain herself from speaking about her experience. She couldn't wait to get Noah alone and tell him about it.

Impatiently, she grabbed Mr. Singh's hand, thanked him profusely, and promised to return again for a visit. She nearly caused Noah to stumble over a chair as she tried to get him moving toward the door.

Mr. Singh sensed something urgent as he, again, politely thanked them for such a privilege to read and decipher the ancient inscription. He hoped they would return soon. "Please don't forget to bring the crystal. Perhaps it could unlock the mystery written here," he said as he pointed to the papyrus Noah was tucking into his backpack.

At the door they each smiled, bowed, and promised to keep in touch.

Hannah could barely wait until they were out of earshot of the house.

"You know, Noah, I didn't tell you what happened when you left to go back to England. Remember how I wanted to keep the crystal and take a good look at it while I was with Mom and Dad?"

"Yeah, I remember. So, what happened?"

Hannah told the story of lying on her bed, and holding the crystal up to her eye.

"I went into a tunnel, and met a spirit being named Light, just like the being you met when you went through the door in the garden wall. Light showed me the history of the earth and how mankind has diverted from the Creator's plan. How we are now to help heal the earth, and bring back the Divine Plan. Light said that our loving, positive thoughts, words, and deeds will raise the mass consciousness and bring Mother Earth into the higher dimension of the original plan. She said there is only one language, and it comes from the heart. There is only one thought, and that is love."

Noah stopped walking and turned toward his sister, hardly knowing what to say. "You mean.. you really met Light? And... you also have experienced the higher wisdom?"

"Oh, yes, if that's what you want to call it. I thought perhaps it was all a dream or something from my imagination. Except...

Noah, I swear I remember it as though it was an actual experience that happened only yesterday."

"I know what you mean. I also remember my experience as though it happened yesterday. Hannah, I am not sure we should take the crystal to Mr. Singh and let him have a look at it. This is getting very interesting, to say the least. We may have the discovery of the millennium right in our hands!"

Hannah spotted a sidewalk cafe and an empty table.

"Let's sit there and have a bite to eat. We can talk this over and decide later what we're going to do. I'm a little concerned about what will happen to the papyrus or the crystal if we try to delve too deeply into this mystery and bring too many people into the reality of its existence."

They settled into their cafe chairs.

"After all," Hannah nearly whispered, "we're talking about a codex possibly from the ancient library of Alexandria, Egypt. Wasn't it burned to the ground hundreds of years ago? Like, in 540 AD? What about the comet hitting the earth fifteen and a half million years ago? And what about Atlantis? All of this is just too spooky for my taste. Mom and Dad don't even know about any of this yet."

"Yeah, you're right. We definitely need to go slowly on this one. It would be really easy to get in over our heads. If it's what it appears to be, we may have to give this up to the government or some cause for the preservation of ancient antiquities or historical artifacts. Let me do a little research and ask around at the university about what options are open to us."

"Great idea," answered Hannah while trying to get the waiter's attention. "Let's order, I'm starved."

When they returned to Arjun's flat that evening, Noah and Hannah decided to go over what Mr. Singh had told them and write it all down in as much detail as they could remember. They decided they should head back to Cambridge to sort things out before any information could leak out about the crystal or papyrus. Noah knew Arjun would question his grandfather about their visit, and he and Hannah wanted to be gone by then.

Just before turning in for the night, Noah asked Hannah to have a look once again at the crystal. Hannah dug through her backpack and located the crystal.

"Here it is. Noah, you take a look into it and see what you can see. I'm tired and I'm going to bed. See you in the morning." She handed the crystal to Noah and went into the small bedroom.

Noah lay down on the sofa, covered himself with a blanket, and leaned back against the pillow. The crystal lay on the table in all of its mystery, appearing like an eye looking back at him. Picking up the crystal, Noah turned it around and around trying to see if one of the facets resembled an opening or window. *Ah, could that be it?* He wondered as he saw a diamond-shaped facet in the middle of the crystal. Holding the crystal up to his right eye, Noah looked into the facet opening. Peering deeper and deeper, he saw a white mist followed by a bluish tunnel with a soft rose-pink light emanating within.

The light became brighter until Noah suddenly found himself standing at the opening of a cave. The cave was at the edge of a beautiful meadow full of flowers and butterflies flitting here and there. Without hesitation, Noah stepped into the opening. The bright sunlight sparkled off the crystal formations in the cave, casting vivid rainbow colors around the opening. The peaceful frequencies beckoned him to step farther into the cave. An unknown source of light reflected varied colors, which seemed to beckon him from one crystal to another until he found himself in a brilliantly lighted room.

"Hello, Noah," a familiar voice whispered.

Startled, Noah quickly turned around. Standing before him was Light, as radiant as he remembered her when he was a little boy.

"Light," Noah said almost breathlessly.

"Yes, we meet again." Light smiled as she spoke to him as if they were old friends reuniting. "I see you have found your way back here through the crystal. You never forgot our meeting, and now, you and your sister are on a quest to discover the hidden source within.

"Souls have come to Earth for millions of years, and spend their Earth life searching for the meaning of their existence. They think something outside of themselves will bring happiness and abundance into their lives. They are always looking to someone or something to be the '*source of*' meaning to them. Even you, Noah. You are filled with anticipation of finding the source to the door in the garden wall, the mystery of the ancient papyrus, and the crystal."

Light held up her hand, gesturing toward the sparkling crystals all around her.

"These are only things. They are concepts within the mind. Yet, they are clues, so to speak, to the knowledge and wisdom within your being. These clues are awakened by reading and by words spoken from others. Even Mother Nature is a wonderful teacher. She shows the process of life from the smallest seed to maturity and the continuing cycle. Clues along the path of life will lead you to your true nature, a child of the Law of One."

Light placed her hands on Noah's shoulders and looked deep into his eyes.

"You came from the Creator and are a part of creation. What urges most humans on is trying to find someone or something to fill the awful feeling of loneliness and the longing to be reunited with perfect love. The longing lies in the desire to return to the perfection of Divine Creation."

Noah stood dumb-struck as he listened and tried to take in what Light was telling him. All of this was unexpected, and there he was in the presence of a being from another dimension.

"Light, I'm feeling a little dizzy from this high frequency. I want to ask you a couple of questions about what Hannah and I have experienced concerning the crystal, the door in the garden wall, and the ancient papyrus I found in my great-grandfather's trunk," he said, looking around for a place to sit down.

"Come, sit here beside me," motioned Light as she led him to a bench of opal-colored crystal. Noah sat down beside her and asked his first question.

"Why did the Creator create such a difficult place for us to live only for us to spend our lives trying to find our way back to our true home or reality?"

Light turned toward Noah. A broad, beautiful smile beamed across her lovely face as she answered. "The Creator likes to play games," she said with a laugh. "Almost like hide-and-seek. He found a wonderful hiding place. A place where He knew mankind would never think to look. Their egos would have them running in every direction trying to find happiness, and all the while, it would be in the spot where they would never think to look."

"Where is that?"

Light placed her hand over her heart.

"We all know the spot. It is in your heart. One has to go into one's heart to find the door that once opened, no man can shut."

"How can you do that?"

"Easy," answered Light. "Sit comfortably and close your eyes. Be still, and know, 'I Am Within.' You will discover it."

Noah sat still, thinking. He knew what she said *maybe* made sense.

"But, Light, what should we do about the door, the crystal, and the papyrus? You know Hannah and I are in a dilemma about this. We haven't even told our parents what we've found or what we've experienced."

"Why didn't you tell your parents about your experience going through the door in the garden wall?"

"Because I knew I'd be in big trouble if my mother knew I had disobeyed her. Most of all, I knew no one would believe my story!"

"And what about Hannah? Why didn't she speak of her experience?"

"I guess she must have felt the same way. She only told me because she knew I had had the experience of meeting you in the Fifth Dimension. Then, Mr. Singh spoke of the mystery of the crystal."

"I am afraid, dear Noah, there are few people who would even listen to what you now have discovered about the crystal or the door. After the disappearance of Atlantis, this concept and knowledge were hidden away from the eyes and ears of humans. Mankind had sunk to such a spiritual low that any such ideas were strictly forbidden. This knowledge was practically eliminated, except from the true seekers. For thousands of years, great souls have come to Earth to teach mankind how they can connect to the Creator. Their words often fell on deaf ears."

Light stood and walked over to a crystal formation and stroked it with her hand. Rainbow colors radiated from the crystal, drawn out by the energy of her touch. Turning toward Noah, she continued.

"I am afraid you and Hannah, as well as your parents, would have a very difficult time trying to convince anyone to believe this mystery. Each individual must find their own clues to life and how to live in peace and brotherhood. These clues you became aware of were meant for you, Hannah, and your loved ones. Others will find their own clues."

Light returned and sat next to Noah. Looking into his eyes she said, "Be content with the treasure you have found within your own garden, and share what you know with those you love. Then it becomes a family legend to be passed down from generation to generation. This is how it has always been done. Remember, there is only one language: the language of the heart. There is only one religion: the religion of love."

Noah rolled over. The clock on the wall chimed three times, waking him. He opened his eyes and sat up. A soft thud sounded as the crystal rolled off of the sofa and onto the floor. Sitting up, Noah rubbed his eyes and looked for the crystal. With the help from the light streaming through the open window from the street lamp, he saw it on the floor near his foot. He picked it up and looked at it in the palm of his hand.

The memory of Light's wisdom was fresh in his mind. He rolled the stone over in his hand, then placed it on the table next to the sofa. Noah laid down, thinking about what he should do with the mysterious objects in his care. He knew what he had experienced was true. That was enough. Tomorrow, he would speak to Hannah about Light's message. He felt certain when she returned home, she would agree to return the papyrus to the trunk and place the crystal back in the door in the garden wall. Most of all, they would share what they knew in their hearts with those they loved. With that in mind, Noah fell into a deep, peaceful sleep.

Noah did tell his parents about his experience of going through the door in the garden wall, meeting Light, and taking the crystal out of the door so he would not get caught in a time warp.

After listening to Noah's part of the story, Dad stood up and said, "I've heard enough! All of this is total nonsense to me!" he pronounced as he stormed out of the room.

The remaining three of them sat in silence, staring at one another.

"Well, that certainly supports my theory of disbelief by others who lack experience in the 'other dimension,'" Noah said, shrugging his shoulders.

Mom and Hannah smiled, nodding their heads in agreement. Then, Hannah related her experience of looking into the crystal, meeting Light, and seeing the fate of the earth.

Mom listened to their stories with an understanding smile. She subsequently told them her own story.

"One day, when I was alone in the garden, I looked into the crystal and realized that the wonderful knowledge I was receiving was not in the crystal or anything else, but the reflection of going within to the very center of my own being, and finding that special place which is in each of us. That place is where your spirit abides; the divine heart made so by the 'breath of life.'"

She shared with them of the times later on, when the door was first placed in her own garden wall, and the time she looked into the crystal. She described the beautiful, enlightening scenes and secrets of wisdom that she experienced from Light. She had also been concerned that no one would believe her story.

"For a moment, just imagine what it would be like if you never lost sight of your spiritual identity, if you were forever aligned and attuned with an infinite source. Your light body is like the sun whose rays sustain life. Just so, the light of the Spirit sustains your being and provides you with the inspiration that feeds your faith and gives you strength to continue upon life's path."

Noah and Hannah sat with their eyes wide open, staring at their mom.

"You mean none of this was as real as we thought?!" Noah gasped.

"Nor as beautiful as when I was in the crystal cave?!" Hannah exclaimed.

"Oh, yes, it was all very real to you, except it really had nothing to do with the crystal. Your mind just slipped into a higher reality, into the spiritual dimension," she answered.

"What about Great-grandmother and her brother's experience?" Noah asked, again, trying to make sense of what he had been told. "Getting caught in a time warp when they went through the door? And my experience?"

"Ah yes, that was another matter, and still is. There are windows of time distortion. It has been known throughout the ages where people have slipped into a time warp, and we're able to go backward or forward in time." Stepping in front of the window and pulling back the white lace curtains, she said, "Look, the door is completely covered with vines and climbing roses. As you can see, the lilac bush stands as a sentinel before it. As for me, I am not willing to take any chances again with the door or the crystal being placed back into the door. The crystal, papyrus, and the journal of

Great-grandfather Ashcroft will be a part of our family heritage to be passed down for generations."

The three agreed. The papyrus was returned to the old trunk, which was taken to the attic. The box with the crystal was placed back on the top shelf of the bookcase in Noah's bedroom.

*S*everal years passed. Hannah married the love of her life. She continued to dance for several years, then opened her own dance studio. A few years later, she gave birth to two beautiful twin girls. She named one Crystal, and the other Lucia.

Noah became a professor of natural science. He traveled extensively, gave lectures, and wrote books on many subjects concerning the planet and nature. He married a lovely woman and they became proud parents of two sons, Michael and Joshua, and a daughter named Olivia after his mother.

Noah and Hannah shared with all those they loved what they knew in their hearts to be true, and the family legend of the "Door in the Garden Wall" still lives on to this very day.

THE END

Epilogue

*N*early a generation had passed. Dad had died some years ago, and now, Noah and Hannah returned to their family home to oversee their mother's funeral. Within a week, the arrangements were made and the internment was over. Once their families and guests said their good-byes and returned home, Hannah and Noah were left alone in the old house to make arrangements for settling the family estate.

Noah and Hannah were semi-retired and had settled down quite comfortably, often traveling or sometimes living abroad for extended periods of time. Their children were grown and busy with families of their own. Now, the time had come to sell the old family house and dispose of their parents' belongings.

Noah and Hannah sat across from each other in the large living room. Hannah sat comfortably on the white sofa stroking the blue and white Chinese floral pattern on the pillows, reminiscing how much their mom loved the pattern. Noah sat across from her in their dad's navy blue winged back chair with a bronze floor lamp shinning over his shoulder. He was pensive, unsure of how to go about the distribution of his parents' heirlooms.

"Well, what do you think, Hannah? What do you think we should do with all of this stuff?" he asked, waving his arms encompassing the living room.

Hannah looked up and gazed around the room, her eyes focusing on a piece of furniture here and there. She shrugged her shoulders. "You know, Noah, I was never a fan of Mom's antiques." "I would just as well let it all go, except for maybe a favorite piece or two. We can have an estate sale, then sell the house," she said rather matter of factly.

Noah was quiet. He unbuttoned his jacket and loosened his tie. He sat there a moment, pondering Hannah's words. He uncrossed his legs and sat up straight.

"I think you are right. Mom has beautiful furniture, but I really have no use for these things either." Leaning on his elbow on the arm of the chair, he said, "I have all that I need, but let's take a look in the attic, and I will go through the things in my old bedroom. We can spend a few days here to be sure we don't miss anything of importance."

Hannah, always ready to get things done, stood up, slipped her feet into her black pumps, and straightened her black and white plaid skirt. "Okay, let's get started," she said.

Hannah had retained her youthful appearance: tall and slim with a straight back from years of ballet. Her face was still pretty even though she had white streaks running through her dark blond hair at the temples.

Noah, as he aged, had put on a few extra pounds, but he still had a youthful face and a boyish grin. His graying hair had receded a bit from his forehead, but his height and broad shoulders gave him a youthful appearance.

Noah and Hannah went upstairs and began to look and sort through drawers, closets, and bookcases, carefully retrieving old journals, photographs, books, and pictures. Noah found the box with the crystal, still on the top shelf of the bookcase in his room. Hannah found the old chest with the yellowed papyrus, manuscript, and letters in the attic. They agreed that they should keep those things together.

Before they sold the family house, Noah and Hannah walked to the end of the garden where the ivy and rose brambles covered nearly the entire wall. Noah reached through the thick green foliage. He was able to uncover a portion of the old door. Hannah helped Noah hold back the branches, and they both looked at the worn splintered gray wood with the old key still lodged in the rusty keyhole, and the opening where the crystal had been. They both stared in silence at the unforgettable sight, and a rush of memories filled their minds. Noah suddenly let go of the branches and stepped back, startling Hannah to release her hold also.

"Hannah, we cannot leave this door here. This is a part of our lives, our family's lives for generations," Noah said, his voice filled with emotion, yet determination. "I will call someone to have it removed right away before we put the house up for sale. I will take this door with me and keep it for as long as I live."

Within weeks, the door was removed from the garden wall, the furniture sold, and the house was on the market for sale.

Hannah took the old chest of contents, with the letters of Captain Ashcroft, and the yellowed papyrus to her house in upstate New York. Noah shipped the door, and took the crystal with him to his home in Ankara, Turkey, where he lived until he died. The door in the garden wall was forgotten and never heard of again.

Until, one day...

Author's Note

*I*n the spring of 1994 while traveling in central Turkey, I came upon a humble village situated near the bank of a winding river. Strolling through the village, I happened upon an old junk dealer's shop built on the corner of two streets coming together to form a V. This shop not only fascinated me because of its odd wedge-shaped construction, but also the unusual pieces of copper and strange odds and ends the old gentleman had for sale.

As I wandered through his dark, dingy shop, something caught my attention. Standing behind a table laden with various pieces of tinned copper and mended bowls, stood an old wooden door carved with strange symbols. About eye level, in the center of the door, was embedded a crystal. My fascination for this door captivated me the entire time I meandered through the shop, sorting through colorful old rugs and richly woven fabrics.

I purchased the door and had it delivered to my home in Izmir, Turkey. After some years of seeing this door leaning against the upstairs bedroom wall, a story began to waft in the ethers to my senses.

One dreary, rainy morning, I reached for a pad and pencil, headed upstairs, and sat in my favorite rocking chair. Sitting in front of the door, I said, "Tell me your story."

I was barely able to write fast enough. The stories flowed one by one, whispering to me from the old door...the door in the garden wall.